BUBBLES

and other stories

Libby Lazewnik

D1300763

Judaica
PRESS

L E S

and other stories

BESTSELLING AUTHOR

LIBBY LAZEWNIK

Bubbles and other stories

ISBN: 978-1-60763-184-2 (hardcover edition)
       978-1-60763-275-7 (softcover edition)

Editor: Miriam Jakubowicz
Proofreader: Hadassa Goldsmith
Cover illustration: Lidia Lewczuk
Internal and cover design: Nachum Shapiro

THE JUDAICA PRESS, INC.
123 Ditmas Avenue / Brooklyn, NY 11218
718-972-6200 / 800-972-6201
info@judaicapress.com
www.judaicapress.com

Manufactured in the United States of America

To my two
newest grandsons

Shmuel
Wainhaus

and

Yosef Simcha
Lazewnik

with tons and tons of love!

CONTENTS

A WORD FROM
THE AUTHOR

Every person is a whole world! That's what our Sages tell us. Just as the sky is filled with millions and billions of stars — each a world all its own — each of us is an entire miniature universe, too.

Now, imagine that all those little worlds were exquisite soap bubbles floating through the air. Lighter than the lightest feather, and tinted in delicate pastel colors, those billions of bubbles would be a beautiful sight to see.

And so are people! Beautiful, I mean. They're filled with light and color and meaning. And when one person-bubble meets another person-bubble, that's when a kind of magic happens. The magic of caring, and friendship, and loyalty. And also — if you're really lucky — the kind of happiness that makes you feel lighter than air ...

But sometimes, before that can happen, people-bubbles have to bounce around for a while. They may bump into things and feel pain. They may drift away from their fellow bubbles and feel lonely. But the goal is always the same — to make ourselves the best people we can be, so that the great, big world around us can be the best world *it* can be.

That's what the girls and boys in these stories ultimately try to do. So turn the page and float away to visit their lives. Enjoy!

Libby Lazewnik

A PILE
OF PEARLS

It was a beautiful Sunday afternoon — perfect for taking a long, meandering walk with my friends. We could window-shop, stop for ice cream, pause for pizza. All of this called for a certain amount of cold cash, which posed a problem for me. I'd already spent that week's allowance and I didn't want to ask my mother for more money.

The next logical step was a visit to my sister's room. Sara Leah is a year younger than I am, but much better about saving her money. I decided to ask her for a small loan to tide me over until my next allowance came through. I tapped on her door, but there was no answer.

I went inside. I knew where Sara Leah kept her purse, and she'd once told me that, in a pinch, I could take what I needed and pay her back later. I opened her desk drawer, took out the purse, and reached for the clasp.

"*What are you doing*?"

The sharp voice behind me startled me into dropping the purse. It fell to the floor with a *thunk*.

"Whew! You scared me!" I put a hand to my heart.

"What are you doing with that?" She ran past me to pick up the purse I'd dropped.

"I needed a little cash, and you always say I should help myself if I need a loan. What's your problem, Sara Leah?"

"*You're* the problem, sneaking into my room the minute my back is turned! Can't a person have any privacy around here?"

"What are you talking about?" I stared at her. "I *always* barge into your room — and you barge into mine! Since when is that a problem?"

Sara Leah pulled herself together. "Sorry, Etti … I'm just having a bad day. I-I think it would be better if you just went away and left me alone right now."

Shaking my head, I walked to the door and did just that.

Back in my own room, I spent some time trying to figure out what had just happened. My sister and I usually get along fine. She's not a moody kind of girl.

But she'd sure been in a mood today! What was *that* about?

It wasn't until about ten minutes later that I remembered that I'd left Sara Leah's room without accomplishing my mission. I still needed that cash. Off I went down the hall, to tap on my sister's door again.

"Hi, Sara Leah," I said, walking in without waiting for an invitation. "I forgot —"

I broke off, eyes popping. My sister was on her hands and knees on the rug, lifting the bed skirt and peering underneath. She whirled around at the sound of my voice — not an easy feat when you're on all fours — and glared at me.

"Again?! Remember what I said about wanting some privacy?"

"But I forgot to take the money. I'm meeting my friends in a little while."

With a face like a thundercloud, she scrambled to her feet and got out an old, threadbare purse. "How much do you need?"

"Could you spare five dollars?"

"Here." She thrust a bill at me.

"Thanks." Curious, I asked, "Why'd you switch purses? This one's falling apart." Maybe she'd decided to keep her change in the other purse. It had certainly felt heavy enough when I'd handled it.

"Is there anything else you need?" my sister asked, ignoring the question.

Stung, I said stiffly, "No. Thanks again." I started for the door.

Before I reached it, I became aware of a funny sound. I glanced back over my shoulder.

Sara Leah was standing in the middle of the room, right where I'd left her. And she was sobbing silently.

I ran back. "Sara Leah! What's wrong?"

"S-sorry ...," she sniffled. "I shouldn't have taken it out on you ...." She cried harder.

"You're crying because you snapped at me?" I was bewildered.

She shook her head. "The purse ..."

"Which purse? What does your purse have to do with anything?"

Silently, she picked up her new purse — the one I'd pulled out of her desk drawer on my first visit. Still without a word, she opened the clasp and held it out for me to see.

I looked inside. What I expected to see was a pile of change: quarters, dimes, and nickels.

What I saw instead was a pile of pearls.

"Are those *real*?"

My sister nodded sadly. "They're from Ma's pearl necklace."

"What happened?"

"I was trying on my new top, and my friend had

mentioned that it would look great with pearls. I don't have any pearls, but I wanted to see how it would look. So ..."

"You went to try on Ma's necklace."

"Yes."

"Without asking permission?" When we were younger, we often liked to try on the things in our mother's big jewelry box. Ma always said we had to ask her permission first, and wait until she could be there to supervise. We were older now, but the rules hadn't changed.

Sara Leah nodded again. "Ma wasn't home. I thought I'd just bring the necklace to my room, quickly try it on with my new top, and then put it back. But the necklace caught on a button, and the string tore, and all the pearls f-fell all over the p-place ..." She was sobbing again.

It was a perfect "I told you so" moment. But Sara Leah looked so miserable that I didn't say it. Instead, I studied the contents of the purse. "There seem to be a lot of pearls in here. Maybe you found them all."

She shook her head. "I'm sure there are at least a few more that rolled away, out of sight. But I can't find them."

I scanned the room. "Did you look behind the desk?"

"How could any pearls have landed there? The desk is all the way across the room from where I was standing."

"Still, it wouldn't hurt to look ...."

"Etti, I don't have all day," she said impatiently. "I have to figure out what to do about this disaster. When Ma comes home ..." She shuddered.

It was time for big sis to gallop to the rescue. "Easy," I said. "You just have to get the necklace re-strung."

She looked at me with wide eyes, her tears forgotten. "Who can do that?"

"Any jewelry store, I think. It shouldn't be too complicated."

"Etti? Would you go with me?"

I'd had a feeling that was coming. Stifling a sigh — and the vision of a fun afternoon with my friends — I nodded. "Let's go right now. I don't know how long the stores stay open on Sunday."

"Thanks, Etti," my sister said gratefully. She scooped up the purse of pearls and followed me out the door.

Mrs. Weiss hummed to herself as she put away the groceries. She'd run into a good friend at the su-permarket, and they'd spent a pleasant few minutes catching up on each other's lives. Her friend had a wedding to attend tomorrow, and she'd asked Mrs. Weiss if she could borrow a certain pair of earrings that she thought would go well with her outfit. She'd be coming by that evening to pick them up.

Still humming, Mrs. Weiss went upstairs to fetch the earrings.

Sixty seconds later, she came hurrying back out of the room, considerably paler than she'd been just a minute before.

"Girls!" She waited. Her daughters seemed to be out. "Boys!"

Her two sons burst out of their room, followed by little Miri.

"What's going on, Ma?" ten-year-old Sruly asked.

"Have either of you seen my pearl necklace?"

"What would we be doing with a pearl necklace?" Sruly asked. Moishy, who was eight, added, "Is it missing?"

"Yes! The last time I wore it, I distinctly remember putting it back on its hook in my jewelry box. And now — it's gone!"

The boys gazed at their mother in surprise and apprehension. Ma was usually pretty calm. Her present agitation was making them very nervous.

"I thought it was a happy day," Miri said wistfully. "But now, it's a sad one." Lately, the four-year-old had started labeling everything, even the kind of day she was having.

The others ignored her.

"We can help you look for it, Ma," Sruly offered.

"Yes … Yes, you do that. Thank you."

Distractedly, Mrs. Weiss rushed downstairs to the phone. She called her husband to tell him that her pearl necklace, the one he'd given to her at their wedding, seemed to have vanished into thin air.

"There's one." Sara Leah pointed at a modest shop across the street.

I studied it. "At least it's open." The last two jewelry stores we'd passed had had a "Closed" sign on the door. "Let's go."

We waited for the light to change and then crossed the busy street. My sister was eager to reach the store, but something was holding me back. I dragged my feet, thinking hard.

"Come on, Etti! Maybe they can restring the necklace while we wait. Maybe we can get it back into Ma's jewelry box before she even notices it's missing!"

"I doubt they'll do it that fast," I said slowly. "They'll probably ask us to leave the pearls and come back another day to pick up the necklace."

"Whatever. Let's just get started!"

I turned to my sister. "I'm a little worried. I-I've never done something like this before. These pearls are valuable. What if those people just take them … and never give them back?"

"Of course they'll give them back. They belong to us!"

"We don't know them. What if they're not honest?"

"Won't they give us a receipt or something?"

"I don't know," I said. "I just have a feeling we should wait until we get the name of a jeweler who has a good reputation. This" — I waved a hand at the modest shop — "could be anybody!"

"Etti, would you stop worrying? I want to get this over with already."

I fixed her with a steely eye. "Do *you* want to take the responsibility for Ma's pearls being gone forever?"

She faltered. "They won't be gone. We'll get them back …."

But she wasn't sure. And neither was I. She was only twelve and I was thirteen. Neither of us had the slightest experience with repairing fine jewelry. Could we take the chance?

As we gazed at each other, we both knew that the decision had been made. We couldn't do it.

"I'll call Aunt Miriam tonight," I promised. "She'll give me the name of a reputable jeweler."

"So we won't be able to give the pearls in until after school tomorrow. This is really going to drag things out …."

I agreed with her. But what choice did we have?

We turned around and started back the way we'd come, in the direction of home.

Mrs. Weiss was beside herself. The moment her husband walked through the door, she rushed over to tell him the news again. He listened to her assurances that she'd definitely put the necklace back the last time she'd worn it. Then Sruly and Moishy came clattering downstairs to report on the results of their search: nothing. There was no sign of the pearls so far.

"I looked, too," little Miri announced. "I don't want it to be a sad day anymore."

"That's very nice of you, Miri," Mr. Weiss said, smiling down at his youngest child. To his wife, he said, "Let's think logically. There has to be an explanation for this." They sat down at the dining room table to try to figure it out — though, the way Mrs. Weiss was feeling, she didn't know if she was capable of any logical thought at all.

Meanwhile, the boys were enjoying their detecting duties. Having searched their parents' room from top to bottom, they decided to turn their attention to the living room. In seconds, cushions were flying and ornaments overturned. Moishy was crawling behind the couch when the front door opened and their big sisters walked in.

"Girls!" Mrs. Weiss called. "Maybe you can help the boys search. My pearl necklace is missing!"

Sara Leah froze — as if she'd turned into a pillar of salt.

Etti turned red, and then white, and then red again.

From behind the living room couch, Moishy shouted, "No pearls here. But I did find that pack of gum you were missing, Sara Leah!"

Sara Leah didn't answer. She was still frozen.

"*I* found three nickels and an almond," Sruly announced, crawling out from under the table. "But no pearls, Ma. Sorry."

"Why would a pearl necklace be under the dining room table?" Mr. Weiss asked.

His son shrugged. "We're looking everywhere."

Mrs. Weiss turned mournful eyes to her husband. "You gave me that necklace when we got married. Your poor parents … They were so happy to get it for me. How am I going to tell them that it's gone?"

"Maybe Tatty can buy you another one just like it," Moishy suggested.

His mother smiled sadly. "It wouldn't be the same. Besides, necklaces like that cost a lot of money."

Slowly, like a sleepwalker, Sara Leah started moving toward the table. "Ma?"

"It's not the necklace itself that I'm upset about," her mother continued, lost in her own train of thought. "It's everything that it represented to me. Every time I'd put it on, I'd remember the special day when I saw it for the first time. Right after our *chuppah* …"

"Ma?"

Sara Leah was right beside her now. From her place by the front door, Etti watched breathlessly.

Mrs. Weiss turned. Gradually, the faraway look left her eyes and they focused on her daughter. "Yes, Sara Leah. What is it?"

Without a word, Sara Leah took her purse out of her pocket. She opened it and held it in front of her mother.

Mrs. Weiss looked inside — and gasped.

Lying at the bottom of the purse was a pile of shining, white pearls.

"Let me get this straight," my father told my sister. "You tried on your mother's necklace without permission, broke it, and were planning to have it restrung?"

Sara Leah flushed, and nodded. "We were hoping to do it today. But we didn't know where we could find a jeweler we could trust. We were going to call Aunt Miriam to ask her and bring it in tomorrow."

Tatty looked at me. "So you were in on this, too, Etti."

I nodded guiltily. I'm older than Sara Leah. I guess I should have known better ....

He turned back to Sara Leah. "And you thought this plan would help *avoid* making your mother upset?"

"I guess I wasn't thinking too straight," my sister said in a low voice. "I just wanted to get it fixed before Ma found out it was missing."

"Why?"

She looked at him in surprise. "I told you. So she'd never even have to know it had been broken in the first place."

"And why didn't you want her to know?"

Sara Leah hesitated. She hesitated some more. Then she hung her head. "So I wouldn't get blamed ..."

"Ah! That's better. Now we're coming to the crux of the story." Suddenly, Tatty laughed. "Trust that wily old *yetzer hara* to convince you that you were doing the right thing — when just the opposite was true! He persuaded you that it would be so much better to just have the necklace fixed before Ma ever found out ... instead of telling her the truth, and taking the consequences."

"I'm really sorry," Sara Leah said to Ma. She looked it, too.

"That's okay." Ma seemed more relieved than upset. "It was an accident, and you tried to rectify it. Next time, though, remember the old adage: 'Honesty is the best policy.' You would've saved me a very difficult couple of hours!"

"I will," Sara Leah said earnestly. "Uh ... I'm not sure I found all the pearls. There may still be a few more, lost in my room."

Ma smiled. "Okay, here's what we'll do. Boys, girls — everyone search Sara Leah's room for the missing pearls. And while you're doing that, your father and I will run out to pick up some take-out for supper. With all the excitement, I never had a chance to think about cooking!"

"Yay!" Miri cried. "It's a happy day again!"

I agreed with my little sister. It *was* a happy day.

Ma had her precious pearls back. Tatty was happy because Ma was happy. My brothers were happy because we were having take-out for supper.

And Sara Leah — well, she was probably happiest of all. It's not easy carrying around a guilty secret. With each passing minute, it can feel heavier and heavier. For the first time since the necklace broke, she was smiling as she ran upstairs to join the search for the missing pearls.

I followed them. I was happy, too — just because everyone else was.

And when Sara Leah came running downstairs to show off her first find, a pearl that had rolled behind her desk — the very place I'd suggested that she look — I didn't even say "I told you so." For the second time that day, I bit my tongue.

Because, apart from the real missing pearls, I guess we'd all picked up a few pearls of wisdom today, too. And here was one that I'd just figured out: There are some thoughts that it's *much* better to keep to yourself!

ACCIDENTS HAPPEN

Mr. Braun hung up the phone and rejoined his family at the dinner table. "That was Uncle Zalmy," he said.

"Oh?" his wife asked. "How are he and the family?"

"The family's fine, *baruch Hashem*. Zalmy had a bit of a mishap on the highway this morning."

The Brauns reacted with horror. "Is he okay?"

"Thank goodness, it was a minor accident. Seems that a car to the right of him lost control, at the same time that a truck to the left of him had a tire blow out. And there was poor Zalmy, stuck in the middle."

"Was he hurt at all?" Mrs. Braun asked.

"Only some minor cuts and scrapes. He needed a few stitches."

The word triggered a memory in one of his children's minds. "Uncle Zalmy once gave *you* stitches. Right, Ta?"

His father laughed. "Yes. The first time I met your Uncle Zalmy, I ended up in the emergency room, where I needed twelve stitches."

"Accident-prone ...," his wife murmured.

"That's right. Zalmy seems to attract accidents the way honey attracts bees," Mr. Braun agreed.

"Tell us about the stitches," his son begged.

"And the cupcakes!" his daughter said.

Everyone in the family knew the cupcake story. That was because their father had been a part of it. In fact, it was because of those cupcakes that he and Uncle Zalmy became friends in the first place.

Mr. Braun never minded telling a good story — and the cupcake story was one of his favorites. Pausing only long enough to eat a little more of his dinner, he put down his fork and launched into the tale.

Zalmy Weinstein was the kind of kid who seemed to land in trouble, no matter how hard he tried to avoid it.

For instance, when he helped clear the table at the end of a meal, it was only by sheerest good luck that he *sometimes* managed to avoid dropping — and breaking — a plate or a glass.

If he had an important paper to bring home from school, half the time it was snatched away by the wind, accidentally thrown in the garbage, or chewed up by a neighbor's dog.

And at the tail end of winter one year, he managed to slip on the last patch of ice in Brooklyn and break his arm.

"All thumbs," people said of Zalmy.

"He has two left feet!" others declared.

His parents just called him "accident-prone."

His mother said this was something unpleasant that he would probably outgrow, like baby fat. His father said that these things happened because Zalmy didn't pay enough attention to what he was doing. And perhaps he was right. Zalmy was often lost in a world of his own, thinking about something other than what was in front of him at the moment. Which could be — and often was — a recipe for disaster.

The first time he met Yitzy Braun was on the day the Brauns moved in around the corner from the Weinsteins.

Because their two houses were back-to-back, with nothing but a few bushes in between, the Weinstein children and those of the house's former occupants had been back and forth between each other's homes all the time. When the Weinsteins came over to welcome the Brauns with a homemade cake on their second day in the new house, Mrs. Braun cordially invited the Weinstein kids to continue the practice.

"Why bother walking all the way around the corner if you want to come over and play?" she asked with a smile. "Just pop on over! Or you can use our yard as a shortcut to get somewhere else. Be our guests!"

Zalmy was eyeing Yitzy Braun, who appeared to be about his own age. Yitzy was eyeing Zalmy right back. Suddenly bashful, Zalmy retreated a step — and stepped on a scooter that someone had left lying there. The scooter started moving down the gentle slope. With a gasp, Zalmy went right along with it. When the scooter hit a bump, off flew Zalmy — right into Yitzy Braun. Yitzy fell down, hard.

There was a commotion as Mrs. Braun and Mrs. Weinstein rushed to Yitzy's side, trying to wipe away the blood that was pouring from a cut in his temple. The episode ended with a trip to the emergency room, where Yitzy was treated to twelve stitches.

Zalmy was mortified. He'd managed to hurt his neighbor before they'd exchanged a single word!

When it turned out that Yitzy was not only registered in his yeshivah, but was actually going to be in his class, Zalmy felt even worse. On the first day of school, he shyly said hello to Yitzy, who responded with a cautious "hi." He didn't seem to want to get too close to Zalmy — and Zalmy didn't exactly blame him.

Yitzy was still wearing a bandage on his injured head.

But even when the bandage came off, Yitzy remained out of Zalmy's reach. His classmates had taken to the new kid, and Yitzy soon had as many friends as he wanted. Zalmy had his own group of friends, too, but it would have been nice to add Yitzy. The two of hem, living so close, could have had lots of fun to-her.

That was the state of affairs on the day Zalmy's r sister, Chana Leah, came home with her ex-_cws.

"Ma! Ma! Guess what?"

Mrs. Weinstein turned to smile at her ten-year-old. Chana Leah was a rather chubby girl with fine, curly hair and round cheeks that looked like red apples when she was excited. She was certainly excited now.

"What is it, Chana Leah?" Mrs. Weinstein asked.

"You know those girls I've been trying to make friends with? Elky and Rivky and Mimi and Tzirel?"

Her mother nodded. Chana Leah's best friend had moved away in the summer, and she'd been struggling to find new friends this year.

"Well, I finally worked up the courage to invite them over on Shabbos. And they said yes!"

"That's great, Chana Leah. I'm so glad for you."

Chana Leah gave a happy twirl around the kitchen. "Can I have a box of chocolate-cake mix, Ma? I want to make cupcakes for when they come. With sprinkles. Okay?"

"No problem, sweetie. It's in the pantry."

Halfway there, Chana Leah changed her mind. "No, I'll make them tomorrow, so they'll be fresher on Shabbos. Will I be able to bake them tomorrow afternoon, Ma?"

Fridays could be hectic in the Weinstein kitchen, but Mrs. Weinstein knew how much this meant to her daughter.

"No problem," she said again. "I'll make sure the oven is available for you when you need it."

"Great! Thanks, Ma!" With a quick hug and another joyous twirl, Chana Leah danced out of the kitchen.

Mrs. Weinstein believed in putting all her kids to work on Erev Shabbos — boys as well as girls. But it was hard finding just the right kind of job for Zalmy. When he was around, dishes tended to break, water to spill, and trash cans to tip over.

The pareve, stainless steel mixing bowl and utensils seemed a safe enough bet. Which was why Mrs. Weinstein told Zalmy, the next afternoon, "When Chana Leah puts her cupcakes in the oven, I want you to wash up after her, Zalmy. Please clean the mixing bowl and measuring spoons and spatula. Okay?"

"Sure!" Zalmy was always ready to help. "Should I mop the floor, too?"

"Uh … how about if you just sweep? I think it's Mindy's turn to mop." Mrs. Weinstein still shuddered at the memory of what had happened the last time Zalmy was left alone with a mop and pail ….

"Okay, Ma."

Chana Leah mixed her cupcake batter. When it was ready, she carefully scooped it into a muffin pan lined with paper cupcake holders, and inserted the pan in the oven. Then she set the timer for eighteen minutes. "I'll be back when they're done," she told Zalmy as she carried the bowl to the sink.

"Hold on!" Zalmy stopped her. "I want to lick that."

"Fine." Chana Leah dumped the used utensils in the sink but left the bowl on the counter for her brother. "See you in … seventeen minutes!" she sang out, and left.

Zalmy decided to start with the sweeping, and then reward himself with the leftover batter on the sides of the bowl before washing it and the rest of the things in the sink. He grabbed the broom and started moving it energetically around the room.

The baking cupcakes were starting to smell awfully good. The aroma distracted Zalmy. Before he knew it, the broom got tangled up with a chair leg, and the chair leg got tangled up with Zalmy's foot. Zalmy found himself on the floor, with the chair on top of him. The broom handle smacked him in the eye. "Ouch!"

Putting the room to rights and getting some ice for his swelling eye took a few minutes. Meanwhile, the cupcakes were smelling better and better. Zalmy had put away the ice and was just finishing the sweeping job — this time, mercifully without mishap — when his sister came back. As if on cue, the timer started dinging.

"Perfect timing!" Zalmy grinned.

Chana Leah was too anxious about her cupcakes to comment. She opened the oven door and peered inside. Very slowly and carefully, she pulled out the muffin pan with oven mitts.

"Beautiful!" Zalmy exclaimed.

"They're perfect," his sister breathed. She set the cupcakes on the counter to cool. "I'll add the frosting and sprinkles when they're not so hot …."

"They look good enough to eat," Zalmy said wistfully.

"Don't you dare! They're for my friends!"

"I was just kidding, Chana Leah. I'm not going to touch your cupcakes."

Reassured, Chana Leah checked the clock. "I'm going upstairs to get ready for Shabbos and clean my room. In about an hour, I'll come down, add the frosting and sprinkles, and put the cupcakes away." That decided, she left the kitchen to Zalmy again.

Zalmy had gone to the sink to wash the dishes when he noticed the bowl sitting on the counter. The batter residue had begun to harden, but that didn't stop him from having a taste.

"Eew!" He'd expected sweet, gooey goodness. Instead, he cringed from the taste.

Chana Leah had obviously done something wrong. Had she confused the salt and sugar? Forgotten some vital ingredient? Whatever it was, it had made the batter most unpleasant.

Which meant that her cupcakes — the special cupcakes that she'd baked for her new friends — would be just as awful …

Zalmy didn't know what to do. His first impulse was to share the news with Chana Leah. He ran upstairs — only to find that his sister was already in the shower. It was getting perilously close to Shabbos. He didn't want to greet her later with the news that her cupcakes had flopped. It would be too late then to do anything about it. He had to do something … now. But what?

He returned to the kitchen and went to the pantry. Yes, there was another box of chocolate-cake mix on the shelf. The directions seemed easy enough to follow. His sister would not be back down for an hour. He could whip up another batch of cupcakes, and Chana Leah would never even have to know ….

But Zalmy was realistic. He had no experience with baking. No matter how easy the directions were, he was bound to mess them up. This was the last box in the pantry. It represented his last and only chance to help Chana Leah.

He thought of something. He shook his head: bad idea.

Then he thought about it again. Maybe it was a good idea after all?

His next-door neighbors in the house on the right were away for Shabbos, and on the other side lived an elderly couple that he didn't want to bother on an Erev Shabbos. But there *was* one other option …

Without pausing to let himself think or get cold feet, Zalmy scooped up the box of cake mix in one hand and the now-cool muffin pan in the other, and scooted out the back door.

Though he and his siblings had an open invitation from the Brauns, this was the first time Zalmy had ever actually crossed his own backyard into theirs. There was a gap between the bushes more than wide enough for him to get through. In less time than it takes to tell about it, he was knocking on the Brauns' back door.

Mrs. Braun opened it, wearing an apron and a

startled expression. "Zalmy! Do you need to borrow something?" Her eye fell on the box of cake mix in his hand.

"No. I — I need your help, Mrs. Braun."

What Jewish mother can resist those words? She opened the door wider and invited him in.

Yitzy wandered into the kitchen about fifteen minutes later — to be met by an astonishing sight. Zalmy Weinstein was standing at the kitchen counter, chatting with Yitzy's mother while she efficiently whipped up a batter.

"What's going on?" Yitzy blurted.

Both his mother and Zalmy turned around. "We're baking cupcakes," Mrs. Braun said calmly.

"But ... why?"

Zalmy hesitated. Then, in quick, shy sentences, he told Yitzy the story he'd related to Mrs. Braun a few minutes before.

"Do you really think your sister won't know?" Yitzy asked skeptically when Zalmy was done.

Mrs. Braun was pouring the batter into the Weinsteins' muffin pan. "I'm going to pop these into the oven right now. They should be ready in ..." She reached for the box to check the directions.

"Eighteen minutes," Zalmy said.

"Eighteen minutes. Then Zalmy will bring these

cupcakes back to his own kitchen to replace his sister's."

"And Chana Leah will never guess what happened!" Zalmy finished happily.

Yitzy thought this over. "I guess it could work … *if* your sister takes a long shower."

"She said she was also going to clean her room. Anyway, she was planning to add the sprinkles in an hour."

"How much time does that leave us?" Yitzy asked.

Zalmy was warmed by the "us." He glanced at the clock. "About thirty-five minutes to go."

"Wanna play something while we wait?"

"Sure!"

"Boys," Mrs. Braun called as they were rushing out of the kitchen, "don't you want to lick the bowl first?"

"*Yes!*"

This time, the batter was everything it was supposed to be. Zalmy licked his spoon with relish, and Yitzy did the same with his.

Then the two boys went up to Yitzy's room to while away the time until the timer dinged.

"Hmm. These cupcakes sure are taking a long time to cool off," Chana Leah said with a frown. She was dressed in her Shabbos robe, her hair brushed and her face shining. "I wanted to put on the frosting and sprinkles, but the cupcakes are still hot. I don't want the sprinkles to melt."

"Give it a few more minutes," Zalmy advised.

"But you'd think a whole hour would be enough time for the cupcakes to cool off!" Chana Leah was still puzzled.

"The kitchen's pretty warm today. Ma's been cooking since the morning ... But I'll tell you one thing, Chana Leah," Zalmy said.

"What?"

"I tasted the batter." He rubbed his stomach. "Your friends are sure in for a treat tomorrow!"

Instantly, the frown vanished from his sister's face. She glowed. Four of her classmates were coming over, and she'd have freshly-baked chocolate cupcakes to serve them. A sweet start to what she hoped would be a very sweet and lasting friendship ...

"And that was the start of my friendship with Uncle Zalmy," Mr. Braun concluded.

"And when you all grew up, Uncle Zalmy married Aunt Rina!" his daughter squealed.

"That's right. He married my younger sister, and in due time your cousins were born. I guess you could say it all started with a dozen cupcakes ... and a boy who didn't want his sister to be sad."

Zalmy might still be all thumbs, and he might have been blessed with the proverbial two left feet. He might still be the most accident-prone person Mr. Braun knew, but his heart was definitely in the right place. He cared enough about people to try to make their lives sweeter whenever he could.

Somehow, when Zalmy Weinstein was around, you ended up feeling like the world was a better place than you'd thought it was.

And *that* was no accident at all!

ODD
NUMBERS

"It's perfect!" Gigi exclaimed. "Ma, I can't wait. My bas mitzvah party is going to be the best!"

Mrs. Friedman smiled. She scanned the list they had been putting together. "There's still a lot of work to do before next Sunday. Don't leave it all till the last minute, Gigi."

"I won't. In fact, I'm going to get started on the invitations right now!" Wearing an eager grin, Gigi was halfway up the stairs before her mother even put down her pen.

Gigi burst into her bedroom and twirled around three times in succession before she felt ready to sit down at her desk. Even then, she kept jumping to her feet to let out some of her excitement. It wasn't every day that a girl turns bas mitzvah, and the party she and her mother had planned was going to be fantastic. Pulling out a sheet of clean, white paper, she began to sketch the invitation that she would give out to the girls in her class. It was a small class, in a small school, but that was just fine. The party would be cozy and friendly and fun. She couldn't wait!

When the invitation looked just the way she wanted it to, she ran downstairs to the computer and switched on the graphics program her father had recently installed. Gigi had a talent for art that she hoped to parlay into a livelihood someday. But right now, she had only one thing on her mind: to design the perfect invitation for the perfect party.

Half an hour later, it was ready. Holding her breath, she printed out one copy to see how it looked.

The printer spat out the page in seconds. Gigi picked it up and studied its bold letters and vivid colors. Perfect!

With a satisfied smile, she printed out eleven more copies.

The next day, Gigi moved around the classroom handing out the invitations. After an admiring look, her best friend, Tehilla, tucked hers into her school bag. She knew all about Gigi's bas mitzvah plans, of course. Her friend made sure to keep her updated as each plan was finalized.

It was at least three months since Tehilla and her classmates had last shared in a bas mitzvah celebration. In the Midwestern town where they lived, the cold season was long and bitter. It was good to have something nice to look forward to in the midst of the endless winter. Gigi's party loomed like a spot of brightness and warmth in a frozen landscape. A week from Sunday … Tehilla couldn't wait.

There was a knock at the classroom door. It opened to reveal the principal. Beside her stood a shy-looking girl with a ponytail and rather scared eyes. Mrs. Resnick introduced her as their new classmate.

"Irina is from Russia," the principal explained, putting a reassuring arm around the girl. "She doesn't speak much English yet, but I'm sure she'll learn quickly — especially if all of you girls are as nice and friendly to her as I'm sure you will be." Her eyes searched the small classroom until they found the student they were looking for. "Tehilla, Irina's family moved into a house just around the corner from yours. I'd appreciate if you would walk home with her this afternoon so that she doesn't lose her way."

"Sure, Mrs. Resnick," Tehilla sang out. "No problem." She beamed across the room at Irina, who offered a bashful smile in return.

Perhaps because the principal had singled her out

to help the new girl, Tehilla felt responsible for her. She made sure that Irina had the right textbook for each of the subjects they learned that day, even though it was clear that she scarcely understood a word that the teachers said. On the other hand, Irina seemed to speak the language of numbers better than any of them. Math class found her answering every question with lightning speed. Gigi was especially admiring.

"I wish *I* could do that," she whispered to Tehilla.

"Well, I bet Irina wishes she could speak English the way you do," Tehilla retorted.

Gigi made a face. "The difference is, Irina will get there one day. But I'll *never* be the kind of math whiz that she is!"

When the last bell rang, Tehilla said good-bye to Gigi in front of their school building. Though they didn't live very far away from one another, their houses were in opposite directions. Irina waited patiently while the two friends chatted. Finally, with a last wave at Gigi — who would be calling her, she knew, the instant they were both home — Tehilla started off down the block with Irina in tow.

Walking in silence felt strange, so Tehilla decided to give her new classmate a little English lesson.

"Tree," she said, pointing at the bare, brown branches swaying in the wind.

"Tree," Irina said obediently, with a tiny giggle.

"Sky."

"Sky."

"Sidewalk."

"Side-volk ..."

She led Irina up to the front door of her new house. As soon as it had closed behind her, Tehilla picked up speed and raced around the corner to her own house. She was chilled through, and more than ready for the hot drink that would be waiting for her in her mother's warm kitchen.

Ten minutes later, hands cradling a mug of hot chocolate and the phone tucked under her chin, she was on the couch chatting with Gigi.

"We decided to go with the theme of the twelve *shevatim*," Gigi chattered happily. "Isn't that perfect? Luckily, when we put the leaves in our dining room table, it holds twelve people without crowding. And as a centerpiece, I finally decided on —"

"Wait a second," Tehilla interrupted. "Twelve?"

"Sure. We've always had twelve girls in our class, remember?"

"Not anymore," Tehilla said slowly.

There was silence at the other end of the phone. Then Gigi said, "Oh. You mean ... Irina."

"Yes. That's exactly who I mean."

"Tehilla, she'll have been in our class just barely over a week by the time I have my party. She doesn't even speak English! She won't know or care that she wasn't invited ...."

"How do you know? Anyway, why can't you just invite her?" Tehilla demanded.

"I told you — the numbers will be off. The theme of the whole party is the twelve tribes. We're planning to give each of the girls the identity of one of Yaakov Avinu's sons. My sister and I figured out a couple of good games and projects based around that theme. And I already told you that our table seats twelve perfectly. Any more, and we'd have to set up a folding table." Gigi ended on a victorious note, as if to say, "I rest my case."

Tehilla tried arguing with her, but her friend's mind was made up. Gigi had worked long and hard planning this momentous day, and the arrival of one Russian girl to their class was not going to be allowed to upset those plans. Nothing Tehilla said seemed to make the slightest dent in that decision.

"Come on, Tehilla. Drop it already!" Gigi was growing impatient.

Tehilla drew a long breath. "Gigi … are you absolutely sure you won't change your mind about this?"

"Positive. I don't know why you're making such a fuss. Irina will never even know about the party."

"I'm not so sure about that," Tehilla said darkly. "She could easily find out. And when she does, she'll be devastated!"

"I doubt that."

"I don't."

"Tehilla, I'm going to hang up now. I'm tired of arguing."

Tehilla was tired, too — but not for the same reason as her friend.

She stared sightlessly at the phone for a long time after she hung up.

The phone rang in the Friedman house. Mrs. Friedman, Gigi's mother, hurried across the kitchen to answer it, wiping her hands on her apron to remove the flour that was on them. She'd been baking Gigi's birthday cake.

"Hello?"

"Hello, Mrs. Friedman? This is Miri Fuchs."

"Oh, hello, Miri. I'm afraid Gigi's not home right now."

"I know. She's gone shopping with her big sister, right?"

Mrs. Friedman was surprised, and then amused. These girls certainly kept tabs on each other.

"That's right," she said. "Do you want to leave a message for her?"

"Yes." Miri hesitated. "Uh, would you tell her that I called to R.S.V.P. for her bas mitzvah party?"

"Certainly. We'll be happy to see you here next Sunday, Miri."

"Uh … that's just it. I can't make it."

"You can't?"

"No. Will you tell Gigi, please?"

"Certainly, Miri. What a pity!"

"Yes," Miri said softly. "It is ...."

Mrs. Friedman was troubled as she went back to her cake. She had been uncertain about Gigi's "twelve tribes" theme — and it looked as though she'd been right. They were down to eleven girls now ....

The phone rang.

It was another classmate of Gigi's — Lana Davidson. She, too, was sorry to say that she wouldn't be able to make Gigi's party. Mrs. Friedman was wearing a slight frown as she hung up and returned to her cake batter.

By the time she'd taken the third, fourth, and fifth calls, the frown had deepened considerably. After the sixth, seventh, eighth, and ninth ones, Gigi's mother was frankly bewildered. The tenth call came right on the heels of the ninth.

And then, after a discreet interval, the phone rang for the final — and eleventh — time. It was Tehilla.

"Tehilla!" Mrs. Friedman exclaimed to her daughter's best friend, who had practically grown up in her house. "You wouldn't believe what's been happening! Nobody can come to Gigi's bas mitzvah party next week! It looks like we'll have to reschedule."

Tehilla drew a deep breath. "Not really, Mrs. Friedman. There *is* another solution."

"What is that?"

"I think that everyone in the class would find that they *could* come to the party — if 'twelve' turned into 'thirteen' ...."

Gigi came home from her shopping trip with her older sister, laden down with party favors, props for the party games, and a brand-new outfit for the birthday girl. Her mood was elated. But it didn't last long.

"*What?!*" she screeched.

"You heard me," her mother said quietly. "Nobody intends to come to your party unless you invite Irina, too."

"This is all Tehilla's doing!" Gigi exclaimed furiously. She stalked over to the phone. Her hands shook with rage, making it hard for her to dial the familiar number. Tehilla sounded nervous as she answered. *As she should be!* Gigi thought, gnashing her teeth.

"So! This is how my best friend decides to celebrate my bas mitzvah!" she started without preamble. "By sabotaging the whole thing!"

"Gigi, I —"

"You *knew* I was having a 'twelve tribes' theme. You *knew* our table seats only twelve comfortably. You *knew* that inviting Irina would mess up the numbers. But you didn't care. Oh, no, not you! You just went ahead and got the whole class to go ahead and — "

"Gigi," Tehilla broke in desperately, "what's more important: the right numbers, or doing the right thing?"

Gigi opened her mouth, and then shut it again. Fury battled with guilt, making it impossible for her to speak. After a few more fruitless grimaces, she slammed down the receiver.

At the other end of the line, Tehilla stared at the silent phone.

I did the right thing, she thought miserably. *So why am I the one crying right now?*

The next morning, Tehilla all but tiptoed into the classroom. She was terrified of meeting Gigi's eyes and finding a stranger looking back at her. They had been friends — best friends — for longer than she could re-member. Losing Gigi's friendship would leave a huge, gaping hole in her life. She could hardly bear to con-template it.

But she hadn't been able to bear what Gigi was doing, either. As she'd told her friend — and as she believed to the depths of her heart — doing the right thing was more important than anything else.

Thirteen girls took their seats as the bell rang. Their teacher walked into the room. Like a flash, Gigi shot up and went over to the front desk. She spoke quietly with the teacher for a moment. Tehilla saw the teacher nod. Gigi said "thank you" and turned to face the class.

There were a few beats of absolute silence. Curious as they were, Gigi's classmates did not say a word. They just waited at the edge of their seats to see what she had to say.

"I would hereby like to issue an invitation to the entire class" — her eyes went to Irina and then, briefly, to Tehilla — "to my bas mitzvah party next Sunday. It's a lunch party, scheduled for twelve noon, and everyone is invited." She paused. "The theme will be 'achdus.' That," she explained for Irina's benefit, "means 'togetherness.' Being all together. United. Understand?"

Whether or not Irina understood was hard to say. But she did, apparently, know the word "party." And it was a word that set her smiling from ear to ear.

But not even Irina's high-voltage beam matched Tehilla's smile, as she caught the birthday girl's eye and gave her a thumbs-up.

And if Gigi's responding grin was a bit sheepish, can you blame her?

Winter still held that little Midwestern town in its icy grip. But the small class had something to look forward to now — a *real* spot of warmth in a frozen landscape.

A hint of glorious summer in the very heart of winter.

ONE
TUESDAY

"Bye, Ma. See you later," Yaakov called, slinging his knapsack over his shoulder and heading for the door. It was a sunny but crisp April morning and he was about to leave for school.

"Not *too* late," his mother said. "Remember, you have a new tutor coming to the house today."

Yaakov froze halfway to the door. "He's coming *today*?"

"Yes. He'll be meeting you on Tuesdays, right after school. So remember: no club meeting this afternoon."

This did not please Yaakov at all. A moment before, his face had been as sunny as the weather outside. Now a cloud came over it. "I don't see why I need another tutor," he grumbled. "I have two of them already."

"One for *limudei kodesh*, and the other for your secular subjects," Mrs. Schneider agreed. "But your father and I decided that you need a special tutor who's an expert in math. This fellow comes highly recommended. So don't be late!"

Yaakov trudged off unhappily to school. He was not what anyone would call a natural student, which meant that the long hours he was forced to spend in the classroom were a form of slow torture for him. Over the years, with some help from his various tutors, he'd learned better study habits and started earning better grades.

Still, school was not exactly what he'd call fun. The fun came afterwards, in the clubhouse that he and his friends had built in the woods behind Shea's house.

Every day after school, rain or shine, the four friends would hike down the forest path to the clearing where the little clubhouse stood. It was nothing much to look at, but to Yaakov and his friends it was a palace. How many happy hours they'd spent inside those four, rickety walls!

But not today, he thought with an inward sigh. This afternoon, he'd have to march straight home the minute the bell rang. He had a tutor waiting.

Without the prospect of a club meeting to sustain him, the day seemed endless. Yaakov *tried* to pay attention. He tried to take notes. He tried not to feel like a prisoner sitting in a jail cell. But it wasn't easy.

He wasn't the only one who was struggling. With the sun shining so brightly outdoors, most of his classmates stared longingly out the window, wishing they could run outside and play.

Finally, just when Yaakov was sure that all the clocks in the school must be broken and that they'd be sitting at their desks forever, the bell rang. There was a concerted rush for the door as thirty boys tried to get outside as fast as they possibly could.

"A perfect day for a walk in the woods, no?" Nachy asked, as his three good friends met him at the door.

Moish and Shea nodded enthusiastically. Yaakov groaned.

"What's the matter, Yaakov?" Shea asked.

"No club meeting for *me* today. I have to run straight home to my tutor!"

"I thought you get tutored *after* supper," Nachy said.

"My two other tutors come then. This is a new one — for math. And he wants to meet me right after school." Yaakov gave a half-hearted salute, like a soldier taking his leave. "See you tomorrow, guys ...."

The others watched him go with compassion. The

very idea of hurrying home to a tutor, when there was so much to do and see in the woods, and so much pleasant companionship to be had in their clubhouse, was enough to make them shudder.

Poor Yaakov …

"Poor Yaakov" made his slow way through the streets in the direction of home. He was so used to taking the route that led to the woods that he had to make a conscious effort to direct his steps anywhere else.

Because he didn't usually walk this way at that hour, he saw many things that he didn't usually see. He glimpsed small children climbing down school bus steps, their mothers beaming at them from their open front doors. He saw women unloading bags of groceries from the trunks of their cars and hauling them into their houses. He saw big girls pushing strollers containing their baby sisters or brothers.

By the time their club meetings wound up, people were usually already indoors, getting ready to sit down to their dinners. Grumpy as he was over missing today's meeting, Yaakov found the walk home interesting, because it was different.

There was something else that was different, too.

He stopped and listened. It was a different sound, coming from behind some bushes that bordered a picket fence.

Someone was crying.

He walked past the bushes and looked over the gate. On the front steps of a modest house sat a young girl and an even younger boy. The boy looked about three and was wearing a *yarmulke* and *tzitzis* that appeared to be brand-new. The girl had on a Bais Yaakov school uniform, but her hair looked unbrushed and one shoelace was untied.

As Yaakov watched, the little boy pulled a slice of bread from a plastic package, took a bite, and made a face. Spitting out the bread, he threw the slice onto the ground and reached into the bag for another one.

It was the girl who was crying.

"No ... no! Don't *do* that, Yak. You aren't supposed to throw bread on the floor!"

The boy bit into another slice, and threw that one away, too. "I'm hungry!"

The girl cried harder. "I know ...."

Maybe it was the boy's name: Yak. Short for Yaakov. He remembered being that young — and that hungry. He wondered why the kid wasn't eating the bread. Why was he taking one bite of each slice and throwing the rest away?

The girl, who didn't seem to be more than seven or eight, lowered her head and sobbed into her knees. Yaakov's heart melted. Where were these kids' parents?

He hesitated for one more second, and then pushed the gate open and walked inside.

It was just a few steps to the stoop where the brother and sister (at least, that was what Yaakov assumed they were) sat.

"Hi, kids," he said, stooping down so that he was at their eye level. "Is there a problem? Maybe I can help."

The girl jumped. She hadn't seen him coming. "We're okay," she said bravely, rubbing her cheeks in an effort to wipe away the tears.

Yaakov turned to her little brother, who had just tossed down another slice of bread. "Hey, don't you know you're not supposed to throw away food? Especially bread! Why are you dumping out that whole package of bread like that?"

"The bread is hard," the child pouted. He appeared close to tears himself. "It's hard like a rock!"

"Well, why don't you go inside and ask your mother for something else to eat?"

At this, the girl's lips quivered, and two more large tears rolled down her cheeks. The little boy screwed up his face as if *he* was determined not to cry in front of a stranger, even if his sister did.

"Well?" Yaakov asked, when no one seemed inclined to answer him.

"Our mother ... isn't feeling well," the girl said at last.

"She didn't give us breakfast, *or* lunch," the boy said pathetically. "I'm s-o-o-o hungry ...."

This didn't sound good. Yaakov's heart went out

to these children. "Can you go ask your mother if she minds my coming in? Maybe I can go to the store for her if she isn't well."

"Mommy's sleeping," the little boy told him. "She keeps sleeping and sleeping!"

Now Yaakov was alarmed. Rapidly, he ran through his options. He could go over to a neighbor's house and see if anyone knew anything. He could ask a passerby to let him use his phone and call his mother.

Or he could go inside and check out the situation.

"Take me to your mother," he said quietly. "I want to help."

The young girl looked undecided. Yaakov was a stranger ... but he was also just a kid. A *frum* kid, wearing a yarmulke, with a hint of *tzitzis* peeking out from under his shirt. And something inside her told her that her mother really did need help.

She stood up and said, "Follow me."

The little boy scrambled to his feet and scampered along beside his sister to the front door. The girl pushed it open. Yaakov followed them inside.

The first thing he saw was a livng room floor strewn with about a million toys that no one had told the kids to put away. The second thing he noticed was the absence of cooking smells. There was no supper bubbling away on the stove, as there should have been at this hour.

The third thing was a woman, lying on the couch.

Though she was covered by a blanket, she shivered continuously. Her eyes were closed and her breathing sounded funny, as if each breath had to push its way through an obstacle course. Yaakov didn't know exactly what this woman had — but it was clear that she had something. She needed help, and so did her kids.

"Excuse me," he said, striding over to the kitchen. As he'd hoped, there was a phone there. He called home.

"Ma?"

"Yaakov! Where are you? Your tutor's due here any minute!"

Yaakov drew a deep breath. "Sorry about that, Ma. But I've got a problem here ..."

"This place is way too quiet without Yaakov," Moish declared.

His friends agreed. Their club had four members, and when even one of them was missing, it just wasn't the same.

"I wonder how he likes his new tutor," Shea remarked.

"Whether or not he likes the tutor," Nachy said, "I'm *sure* he doesn't like having to miss our club meetings every single Tuesday!"

Nachy didn't look too thrilled about it himself.

"Maybe we should stop in on the way home, just to say hi," Shea suggested.

"It'll be late by then," Moish said. "My mother expects me home for supper."

"Me, too," Nachy said, and Shea nodded as well.

"Oh, well." Nachy reached for the pitcher to pour himself a drink. "I guess I'll give him a call this evening and see how he's doing."

Nachy was a boy who rarely spoke idly. When he decided to do something, he did it. That night, right after supper, he went to the phone and dialed Yaakov's number.

Yaakov's mother answered. To Nachy's surprise, he heard the sound of young children's voices in the background. Had Yaakov's cousins come to visit or something? Nachy hadn't even known that Yaakov *had* cousins in town ....

"Hi, Mrs. Schneider. This is Nachy. Can I please speak to Yaakov?"

"Oh, hello, Nachy. He's a little busy at the moment — playing a heated game of checkers. I'll see if I can pry him away ...."

A moment later, Yaakov came on the line. "Hi, Nachy. What's up?"

"What's up with *you*? Who're you playing checkers with?"

Yaakov laughed. "It's a long story ...."

"I have plenty of time." Nachy was curious. He sensed a mystery here.

A young voice piped up, practically in Nachy's

ear. "Yaakov! Let's finish our game!" And then a second voice — this one a girl's — asked, "Could I please have some more hot cocoa?"

"Whoops! Gotta go, Nachy. Sorry ..."

"But what about that story?"

"Tomorrow," Yaakov promised. "I'll tell you guys at recess."

Nachy had filled in their other friends, so that by the time they gathered around Yaakov at recess, they were curious, too. Who were the kids who were playing with Yaakov after supper last night? The whole thing seemed very mysterious — and very unlike Yaakov, whose day was usually extremely structured, from the moment he woke up until his last tutor had left and his homework was done at night.

"So?" Nachy asked impatiently. "What's up, Yaakov?"

Slowly, with many stops and starts, Yaakov told his story.

"I don't know why I did what I did," he confessed. "I mean, I don't usually go barging into strange people's houses like that. But those kids looked really miserable ... and something in my heart told me that they needed help."

"What happened after you called your mother?" Moish asked.

"At first, she was mad at me for not coming straight home. But after I explained what happened, she got in the car and came right over. I gave her the address where I was, and on the way she called Hatzoloh and asked them to meet us there."

"Hatzoloh! What did they do?" Nachy asked eagerly.

"They checked out the kids' mother and said they had to take her to the hospital."

"What's wrong with her?" asked tenderhearted Shea.

"Pneumonia ... Anyway, she's in the hospital and starting to respond to the medicine they gave her. The lady's husband spoke to my mother on the phone this morning."

"That's right — what about the kids' father? Where was *he* during all of this?" Nachy wanted to know.

"Seems he's on the road a lot. He's a salesman. Yesterday, he was somewhere in Ohio. After the paramedics took the woman to the hospital, my mother and I went next door to speak to the neighbors, and they gave us his number. My mother finally managed to reach him. Apparently, his wife never even told him she was sick. She didn't want him to worry ... After my mother called, he got on the first plane home."

"And the kids?" Moish asked.

"The neighbors we spoke to were on their way out to a family wedding, and the ones on the other side of their house weren't home. So my mother and I packed a few things for them and took them home to our house!"

"To while away the time with checkers and hot cocoa," Nachy grinned.

Yaakov grinned back. "It's been a while since I did that kind of thing. But the kids were worried about their mother. I wanted to distract them ...." He shrugged.

"You're a hero, Yaakov!" Shea declared.

Yaakov didn't feel like a hero. He just felt like a kid who'd stumbled across something on his way home from school, and tried to help out.

Later, as they sat in their clubhouse, Yaakov found his thoughts going back to yesterday's excitement.

"You know, I just thought of something," he told his friends. "If I hadn't been walking home from school yesterday afternoon, instead of going to the clubhouse as usual, I never would have seen those kids."

"That's right," Nachy agreed. "I guess now you know why you had to have a tutor on Tuesday afternoons."

Moish had an objection. "But what about all the rest of the Tuesdays this year? Why does he have to miss *all* those club meetings just because of one Tuesday when he got to help someone out?"

"Here's the thing," Yaakov said slowly. "This morning my mother told me that my new math tutor contacted her late last night, after I'd already gone to bed. Apparently, his schedule changed. Instead of meeting me before supper on Tuesdays, he's going to have to come later ...." He looked at his friends. "... after supper."

His friends stared back at him.

"So you had to walk home early on just *one* Tuesday?" Nachy asked.

Yaakov nodded. "Because just one Tuesday was necessary, I guess ..."

Shea whistled. "Talk about *hashgachah*!"

And they did talk about *hashgachah*, until it was time to end their meeting and head for home.

One Tuesday.

One family in trouble.

And One Hashem, to make sure they got the help they needed!

WEIRD HOUSE

Who would have thought it was possible for a person's heart to go up and down so many times in a single conversation?

When our teacher reminded us that we were having a big test in two days' time, my heart tumbled in panic.

Then I thought about Hudi, and it soared with hope.

Hudi was a new friend of mine ... Well, actually, an almost-friend. She was a newcomer to our class, and right from the start I'd marked her as someone I'd like to know better. My former best friend had switched schools, and I was in the market for someone to take her place. It's lonely going through school — not to mention the weekends — without someone to share things with.

At the thought of asking Hudi if she wanted to study together, my heart fluttered with excitement — and nervousness. I wasted no time. Almost before the bell rang, I was out of my seat and cutting across the room to the row where Hudi sat.

"Hi!" I beamed.

She smiled back a little shyly. "Hi, Minna. What's new?"

"That humongous test we're having the day after tomorrow." I made a face and shuddered.

"I'm terrified, too," she agreed, starting to pack her notebooks in her knapsack.

"Wanna study together?" I held my breath.

Hudi's face lit up. "Sure! Maybe we could even have a sleepover."

Now my face was as shiny as hers. "Great idea!"

I'd once walked into Hudi's house for a minute when she had to pick something up. It was a perfect-looking place — spacious but friendly, beautifully decorated but comfortable. I would *love* to have a sleepover there with Hudi! I pictured us in her pretty room, studying for a while and then schmoozing the night away. My heart climbed into the stratosphere.

Hudi stood up, slung her knapsack over her shoulder, and smiled at me. "So, wanna have a sleepover at your house tomorrow night?"

That was when my heart thudded to the floor, like a ton of falling bricks.

To understand why it dropped so hard, you'd have to see my house.

All the way home, I pictured it in my mind's eye — and, believe me, I didn't like what I saw.

Over and over, I wished that Hudi had suggested a sleepover at *her* house. But she, apparently, was as eager to spend the night at my house as I was to spend it at hers. And once she suggested doing it at mine, how could I say "no"?

So I said "yes" — and spent the whole way home worrying.

Why was I worried? If you saw my house, you'd know why.

Stepping through the front door, I surveyed the place as if I'd never seen it before. Things I was so used to that I hardly noticed them anymore seemed to stand up and punch me in the eye. With rising trepidation, I started taking a tour.

First, the living room. I stared in dismay at a sofa cushion with the stuffing coming out. At the bare patch on the rug. At the fifty million or so toys littering that rug, and just about every other surface in sight.

With a sigh, I continued my tour into the dining

room. I took note of the broken drawer in the break-front, the scratches on the wooden floor, and the crooked shade at one of the windows. Not to mention the mismatched plates and silverware lying on the table, ready for our dinner. I clenched my fists and looked away.

Next … the kitchen.

"Hi, Ma," I said glumly, standing in the doorway to take in the whole room at once. I saw the scorch mark on the counter where someone had once put a hot pot down, the threadbare kitchen towels that my mother had never gotten around to replacing, and the counters overcrowded with flowering plants, gadgets, envelopes, knick-knacks, mismatched small appliances, and bottles of spices that didn't fit in the spice cabinet. I groaned.

"Are you okay, Minna?" Ma glanced at me as she reached for one of the spices on the counter. A vigorous shake over the pot made whatever was cooking smell even better. But I had lost my appetite.

"I'm fine," I said, though that was far from the actual truth. "Ma, can Hudi sleep over here tomorrow night? We have a big test to study for."

"Of course!" Ma smiled at me. "It'll be nice to finally meet this new friend of yours."

I didn't even want to picture that meeting. It wasn't my mother I was embarrassed about — it was the whole house. With a stifled sigh, I left the kitchen and trudged up the stairs. As I went, I imagined that

I was Hudi, taking things in for the first time. What would she see?

The stickers that my little brother used to line the banister when he was bored one day ... the crayoned pictures my sister had Scotch-taped crookedly onto the wall outside her room ... the scratched paint on my bedroom door. Pushing it open, I stood in the doorway, surveying my domain through Hudi's eyes.

The rug in here was as threadbare as the one in the living room, so that it seemed to be made up of light and dark patches. The linen on my bed was older than time, the color so faded that you could hardly tell what it was supposed to be. Scattered across the bedspread were eight or ten raggedy stuffed animals that I didn't really need anymore but had never had the heart to throw away. The mattress sagged in the middle because I always meant to flip it over, like Ma told me to, but I always forgot. Ditto for the mattress of the high-riser that Hudi would be sleeping on ...

Turning to close the door, I saw a crack running down the middle of the full-length mirror that hung there — a souvenir of the night my sister had sleepwalked right into it. I was gazing bleakly at that crack when there was a tap on the door. My brother poked his head in.

"Yes?" I snapped.

"Ma says supper's ready."

"Okay." My tone said, *Leave me alone.*

He took a closer look at my face. "What's the matter, Minna? Your face looks ... weird."

"It's this *house* that's weird!" I burst out.

He looked around. "Really? Looks like a normal house to me."

I let out an anguished yelp and closed the door so quickly that my brother had to jump back to avoid having it close on his foot.

A second later, the door opened again. Cautiously, he stuck his head back in. "Are you coming to supper?"

"I'm coming, I'm coming!"

"Why are you in such a bad mood, anyway?"

I moaned. "You don't want to know ...."

I did what I could.

That evening I cleared the toys out of the living room — though I suspected that, by the next afternoon, they'd be right back there again. That's what happens when you have five little brothers and sisters whose favorite place to play is smack in the middle of everything.

I tried tidying the kitchen counters for a while, before giving up. Up in my room, I turned over both mattresses and hoped that Hudi wasn't a sensitive sleeper. I even tried taking down the full-length mirror, but it was firmly fastened to the door with screws.

It was no use. My whole house was hopeless.

And after tomorrow, Hudi would know it, too.

Hudi chattered brightly as we walked home the next day. Normally, this would have made me very happy. She was usually pretty quiet, so I was glad she felt comfortable enough to open up with me. But all I could think about was my weird house. If only we were on our way to Hudi's house instead … But what was the point of dreaming?

I opened the front door and walked in ahead of her, moving cautiously as though entering a war zone. The breath I'd been holding rushed out in a long, disappointed swoop. The toys were back on the livng room floor, even messier than before. Last night I'd stuffed the torn cushion behind some others, but it was out in full view again, front and center. The threadbare patch on the rug seemed to scream, "LOOK AT ME!"

I led Hudi into the kitchen to meet my mother. I saw my friend take in the scene — cluttered counters, scorch marks and all.

"Hello, Hudi," Ma said with a big smile. "I'm so glad you could make it! I hope you like meatballs and spaghetti?"

"I love them," Hudi assured her. I was sure she'd have said the same thing no matter what Ma was serving. Hudi is a very polite girl.

I led her upstairs. I could almost feel her noting every grubby sticker along the way. The scratch on my bedroom door seemed even darker than usual.

Pushing open the door, I let Hudi step inside ahead of me. I'd changed the linen to a slightly less faded set, but you couldn't avoid those sagging mattresses. With a sigh, I closed the door, praying that Hudi wouldn't notice the crack — but knowing that there was no way she'd be able to avoid it.

"Wanna study a little before supper?" Hudi asked.

I sighed again. "Whatever …"

All through supper, I kept seeing things through Hudi's eyes.

The meatballs were delicious, but nothing could be tackier than the mismatched plates they were served on. Like a magnet, my gaze kept going to the broken breakfront drawer and the crooked window shade. Seeing them through Hudi's eyes made every-thing seem twice as bad. My heart seemed to drag on the floor as I twirled spaghetti around and around my fork and wondered what Hudi was thinking.

After we'd helped clear the table, Ma shooed us upstairs to start studying. "I'll take care of the dishes tonight," she told me. "Good luck, girls!"

I felt as if I needed all the luck I could get.

By this time, Hudi had had plenty of time to take a good, hard look at our house. She must have been feeling thoroughly disgusted. She was probably wishing she was alone in her beautiful room at home, instead of here in my weird house with me ....

"He-llo-o? Earth to Minna!"

I blinked. "What?"

"I don't think you heard a word I just said!" Hudi teased.

"Sure, I did. Uh ... well, maybe not every word."

"So let's go through it again." Hudi flipped to the previous page in her notebook and started talking.

I hardly listened. I was picturing the moment when she'd get into bed and notice the faded linen and feel the sagging mattress. I was wondering if she'd seen the window shade askew in the dining room, and the scratches on the floor. How could I be expected to keep my mind on what we were studying when I knew that our budding friendship was doomed — and all because of my dumb house?

"Minna? Are you okay?"

Everyone, it seemed, had been asking me that lately. My mother, my brother ... and now, Hudi. I scowled at her. "I'm fine. Why do you ask?"

"Um ... because you look upset."

"You probably wish you weren't here." I jumped up and started pacing the room. "You probably wish you could just go home right now."

"What? I thought we were having a sleepover!"

"You don't have to be polite," I said doggedly. "If you want to call your parents to come get you, I'll understand. It's okay."

"*What's* okay? Who said I want to go anywhere?" Hudi was bewildered.

"You'd better do it now," I said dully. "Go ahead — call home."

Hudi's lower lip began to tremble. "Do you want me to go?"

"Of course not. I'm just trying to give you a way out."

"But I'm not looking for one!"

We stared at each other. I walked over to my bed and sat down with a thump on my sagging mattress. "Tell me the truth, Hudi. You hate my house, don't you?"

She gaped at me. "Why should I hate it?"

"Because it's weird! This place is nothing like your house. Your house is stunning! It's neat, and pretty, and everything m-matches ...." To my horror, I felt my eyes fill.

Hudi came to sit next to me. Even through the blur of tears, I could see that her expression was troubled.

"I'm not sure what this is all about, Minna. I don't hate your house at all. I think it's charming. It's got lots of character."

I gave her a watery smile. "You're just saying that to be polite."

"No, I'm not. I *like* being here. Why won't you believe that?"

"Because," I said, "seeing how weird my house is,

it's hard to believe you'd want to be friends with me ..."

Hudi looked puzzled. "Why? You're not your house, Minna — and your house isn't you!"

It took her quite some time to convince me that she really meant what she was saying. Hudi didn't dislike my house — in fact, she got a kick out of it. But even if she hadn't liked my house, that wouldn't make her like me any less.

You're not your house, Minna.

Why hadn't *I* thought of that?

We talked for so long that we didn't get much sleep that night. Somehow we dragged ourselves out of our sagging beds and got ready for school. We'd arranged for Hudi's mother to drive us. As we stood waiting for her by the front door, Hudi remarked, "I have to warn you — my mother's car looks like it came out of a museum. Talk about *old*!"

"I don't mind old cars," I assured her.

"It doesn't have automatic doors *or* windows. It looks like something our grandparents used to drive. My father's always urging her to get something newer, but my mother says there's still plenty of life in that old car ...."

There was a honk outside. Peeking out, Hudi said, "There it is now." She looked worried.

I pulled open the door and called good-bye to my

mother. We went outside. There at the curb was the out-dated, dilapidated vehicle she'd been telling me about.

"Relax, Hudi." I grinned. "Remember — you're not your car!"

Her eyes widened. Then, slowly, she started grinning back at me.

And then my friend and I turned our backs on *my* weird house and started running toward *her* weird car.

And my heart flew right up to the clouds.

PARTNERS

On the night Feivel Kleinman turned thirteen, the stars were very bright in a deep-black sky.

"You're a bar mitzvah now," his father said, smiling. "Come, Feivel. Let's take a walk."

Feivel's heart started beating faster. His father was the *rav* of their small town in Poland and had very little time for such luxuries as taking walks. Whatever hours were not taken up with community affairs found Rabbi Kleinman sitting at the table in their modest house, a big *gemara* open in front of him.

"Have a nice walk," Feivel's mother called from the stove, where she was cooking something that was sending up a delicious aroma. "I'll have a good meal waiting for my *two men* when you get back."

Feivel felt a flush of pride. He was a bar mitzvah! And his father wanted to take a walk with him. Just the two of them, walking and talking together. It was the best present he could ever have asked for.

They put on their overcoats because it was autumn and the nights were turning colder. Rabbi Kleinman steered his son leftward, away from the huddle of houses that formed the Jewish section of the town, and toward the river. Feivel liked the river during the daytime, when the sun made a thousand diamonds dance on the surface of the water. At night, he *heard* more than saw it: a wide, dark expanse that whispered past his feet.

"This is a milestone," his father said, breaking the peaceful silence. "Becoming a bar mitzvah is the first step in taking your place among Klal Yisrael, Feivel. You can be part of a *minyan* now. This Shabbos, you'll be called up to the Torah for the very first time. How do you feel?"

Mostly, Feivel felt happy. Walking along the riverbank with his father was like a dream come true. He was also excited. A whole new world was about to open up in front of him. He was no longer a little boy, content with childish games. This was serious. This was real.

But that made him feel frightened, too. He looked up at his father, glad that the darkness hid his worried eyes.

"It's ... it's not so easy being a Yid, Father," he said in a near-whisper. "The *goyim* hate us. When my friends and I walk through the streets of the *shtetl*, I can feel their eyes, burning holes in me ...."

"The *goyim* will always hate the Yidden," the *rav* said soberly. "It's been that way since the days of Yaakov and Eisav. But don't be afraid, Feivel. *Chazal* tell us that Hashem will never abandon our nation. '*Yisrael v'Oraisa v'Kudshah Brich Hu — chad hu!*' The Jewish people, and the Torah, and Hakadosh Baruch Hu — are one!" In the darkness, Feivel could just make out the gleam of his father's smile.

"As long as we remain faithful to the Eibishter and keep His Torah, Hashem will be with us. With such a Partner, how can you be afraid?"

Secretly, Feivel was still a little afraid. But his father's words gave him fresh courage and hope. It was scary, living among gentiles who would just as soon kill him as look at him — but Hashem was his Partner. Hashem would protect him ....

At that moment, as if to underscore the thought, the door of the tavern fronting the river opened up, spilling yellow light and the sound of raucous voices into the quiet night air. Three Poles stumbled outside, laughing and swearing. The door closed behind them, and the light was blotted out. But not before the three men spotted the Jewish father and son.

Feivel closed his eyes for a minute, hoping with all

his might that the men would pass them by. But when he opened them again, he saw that the trio of drunken peasants was moving directly toward them.

That was when the dream ended, and the nightmare began.

"Want me to finish them off, Aleksy?" asked Konrad, the tallest and sturdiest of the three Poles. He looked down at the bleeding rabbi and the boy cowering beside him. He was almost sorry they were down. It had been so much fun pummeling them ….

Aleksy, the unofficial leader of the three, was about to say yes when he had an inspiration.

"No," he said slowly. The cold air had driven away some of the alcohol fumes from his brain, helping him to think more clearly. "I have a better idea."

"What?" Gustaw, the third member of the group, asked eagerly. Konrad balled his hands into huge fists, hoping for more violence.

"Do either of you know Jan Stanislaw? He has a small farm on the outskirts of town."

"I know him," Gustaw volunteered. "Didn't he leave town not long ago?"

Aleksy nodded. "He was working for the Duke, and he … got into some trouble. He had to leave in a hurry."

"So?" Konrad was impatient. "What's that got to do with us?"

Aleksy turned to him. "Jan's house is empty right now. Pick up the rabbi, you two. I'll keep an eye on the boy."

"We're going to carry him all the way to Jan's farmhouse?" Gustaw complained, struggling to lift the *rav*'s legs while Konrad picked him up under the arms. "Why?"

"Why do you think?" Aleksy said softly. He grabbed Feivel's arm and pulled him roughly to his feet. "Everyone knows that the Jews revere their rabbi. They'd do anything to get him back, safe and sound. Right?"

"Anything?" Gustaw repeated, as the group began its slow march toward the outskirts of town.

"Anything," Aleksy repeated firmly. "By this time tomorrow, boys, we'll be wealthy men."

Hearing this, his two cronies' faces lit up. The farmhouse was almost a mile away. They picked up the pace.

Suddenly, Konrad turned around. "What if the Jews can't raise the money?" he asked. "What then?"

Aleksy shrugged. "Use your imagination, Konrad. And your fists ... or your knife, if you prefer."

Feivel's heart lurched painfully, until it hurt even more than the arm being held in Aleksy's cruel grip.

By the time the Poles and their captives reached the abandoned farmhouse, the moon had risen. Behind them, the town was asleep — except for the tavern, where the lights still blazed. Gustaw wished he were back there, quenching his thirst with some cheap wine, instead of out here in the cold, lugging his heavy burden. His feet hurt, his back hurt, and his mood had turned sour.

Aleksy opened the farmhouse door and shoved the boy in ahead of him. "We'll put them both in the back room," he decided. Gustaw felt ready to drop. Konrad, who'd been helping to carry the rabbi all this way, hardly even seemed to be breathing hard. This made Gustaw even grumpier.

To relieve his feelings, he threw open the door and dropped the rabbi roughly onto the floor. Konrad, right behind him, followed suit. The instant the pair was out of the room, Feivel ran over to crouch beside his father.

Rabbi Kleinman had a gash across his temple, which was oozing blood down one side of his face. Feivel had been beaten, too, but he'd fared better than his father. As he reached into his father's pocket to find a handkerchief, he noticed that his father's arm was lying at a strange angle. His elbow seemed to be facing the wrong way. Feivel was dabbing carefully at the cut, glad to see that it wasn't too deep, when his father opened his eyes.

"Feivel," he whispered hoarsely, "are you all right?"

"I'm fine, Father." Feivel squeezed back tears of relief. "How do *you* feel?"

The *rav* took a moment to consider the question. "Not too good," he said at last, trying to smile. "But I'll live, I think …"

"Father, those Poles want to keep us here until the *kehillah* pays a ransom!" Feivel tried to clamp down his panic.

"Well, at least that kept them from killing us, *baruch Hashem*." The *rav*'s eyes scanned the small room. "I'm afraid I'm not going to be of much use for a while. My head … and I think there's something wrong with my arm."

"There is, Father. It's all crooked."

Rabbi Kleinman glanced down at his arm and winced. "Look around, Feivel. Try to find a way for us to escape from here."

Swallowing a sudden lump in his throat, the boy turned away and began to study the small room.

By the light of the moon shining through the lone window, he saw that it had been used to store odds and ends. There was a scarred old dresser, a creaky rocking chair, and a broken stool with only two legs. He tried the window but it was sealed shut. The room had only one exit: through the door.

He tiptoed to the door now and listened. Two of their captors were in the front room, exchanging an occasional word. He didn't hear a third voice. He guessed that Aleksy, who seemed to be the smartest of the three, had returned to the town to inform the leaders of the *kehillah* of their capture and to demand a hefty ransom if the Jews wanted the rabbi and his son returned to them alive.

Feivel looked back. His father lay where the men had left him. His eyes were closed again, his face tight with pain. Feivel clenched his fists in fear and helplessness. There seemed to be no way out.

"Look again," the *rav* whispered. The mere act of speaking seemed to tax his strength.

So Feivel looked again. He tested the window again (sealed) and the door (still locked). Then he began to inspect the walls and floor.

In one corner, a puddle of moonlight showed him a faint discoloration. The wood in this part of the floor was slightly lighter than the rest, as though the original planks had been ripped up and newer ones laid down in their place. Looking even more closely, he discerned a narrow crack in the wood. The crack ran around two planks, meeting at the wall to form a square.

He searched until he found what he was looking for: the third leg of the broken stool. Thrusting one end into the crack, Feivel used it as a lever to pry up the first of the newer planks. It came up with surprising ease, as if someone had done this before. Then he did the same to the second plank. He stood up, peering down into the hole beneath the removed lumber.

There was something in there. Something that gleamed faintly in the moonlight. Feivel reached in and pulled out … a wine bottle. Turning it to face the window, he saw a coat of arms stamped on the side.

He was holding a bottle of the Duke's wine.

"How many bottles are there?" Rabbi Kleinman whispered. Each word cost him an effort.

"I counted a dozen, Father. One full case. But there may be more below that. I couldn't reach that far."

"The Duke's wine," the *rav* mused out loud. "Now I understand why Jan Stanislaw, the owner of this house, had to flee for his life. If it was discovered that he'd been stealing wine from the Duke's cellars …"

"How can this help us, Father?" Feivel asked in despair. What good was a bunch of wine, however fine it was? They still had no way out.

"Remember your Partner, Feivel," his father said softly. "*Daven* to Him now. *Daven* as hard as you can."

"And then?"

"And then …" For the first time, the *rav* smiled. "Come back to me. I'll tell you exactly what to do."

Gustaw and Konrad were sitting with their feet on the kitchen table, chatting in a desultory way and trying not to fall asleep, when a sudden commotion from the inner room made them whip up their heads. It sounded as if someone was turning the room upside down!

In two steps, Gustaw was at the door. He thumped fiercely, shouting, *"Stop that noise!"*

The noise continued, unabated. Furniture was being overturned and things were being tossed. What was going on in there? Were the prisoners trying to escape?

Cursing under his breath, Gustaw fished the key out of his pocket and turned it in the keyhole. He pushed the door open and stalked in, Konrad right behind him. Both of them were ready to give these Jews a sound beating for putting them to the trouble of getting up.

"What's going on here?" he roared.

Feivel was crouched in the corner. The room looked as if a hurricane had swept through it. Except for the wall against which the rabbi lay, the place was littered with overturned and broken furniture.

Konrad pushed his cohort aside and approached the boy. He reached down to pluck the youngster up by his collar. It wouldn't do to hurt the boy *too* badly — not until Aleksy returned to tell them whether the Jews had agreed to pay the ransom. But a good shaking would leave no mark ...

As Feivel flew into the air, dangling at the end of

the Pole's strong arm, Konrad glanced down. His eyes widened. "Gustaw! Look at this!"

Gustaw was at his side in an instant. "What ...?" He stopped in mid-sentence, his own eyes growing round.

In a hole beneath the floor lay ... a full case of wine! Gustaw stooped to pick up a bottle. At once, he noticed the coat-of-arms engraved on the side.

"The Duke's wine," he breathed.

Both men stared at the wine for what felt to poor Feivel like an eternity. He squirmed. Absently, Konrad dropped him. He stared, enraptured, at the bottle in his friend's hand.

"I've heard about the Duke's cellar," he said. "They say there's no finer wine in the district."

Gustaw and Konrad looked at each other in sudden excitement.

"Who's to know?" Gustaw murmured.

Konrad guffawed. "No one — that's who!"

With that, he reached into the hole and pulled up the entire case of wine, as easily as a baby might pick up a toy. The two men left the room, closing and locking the door firmly behind them.

And the party began.

Two hours later, when Aleksy returned, flushed with triumph, he found his two partners in crime snoring at the kitchen table, sound asleep. The three empty wine bottles beside them told their own story.

With a muffled oath, Aleksy grabbed the key from Gustaw's pocket and ran to the back room.

It was empty.

Shards of glass lay scattered beneath the window. A wooden stool with a missing leg had been used to smash it. How the boy had managed to get his father over the windowsill and out the other side, Aleksy would never know. It must have been quite painful for the rabbi. But, painful or not, both the rabbi and his son were gone — and with them, any chance of getting the ransom he'd been hoping for …

He ground his teeth in frustration and anger. With a furious shout, he rushed back to the front room. He wanted to pick up one of the empty bottles and smash it over his companions' heads.

But there was still more than half a case of wine on the floor beside them. Where had it come from?

Curious, Aleksy stooped to pick up one of the bottles. He saw the Duke's emblem and put two and two together, just as the *rav* had.

He hesitated. He could chase after the runaway captives and try to bring them back — though, by now, they were undoubtedly far away from here. Or he could pursue his first plan and smash a bottle over someone's head to relieve his feelings.

But there was a third choice. He could have a taste

of the finest wine he would ever enjoy in his lifetime ...

He hesitated no longer. With a shrug, Aleksy sat down at the table beside his slumbering partners and poured himself a glass.

The way home was long. Correction: The way home was endless. Feivel supported his father as best as he could, but the pair made slow, staggering progress.

To while away the time — and chase away their fears of being pursued — they continued the conversation they'd started hours before, along the riverbank.

"Tonight, Feivel, you saw the difference between a Yid and a Polish peasant. When a Yid finds himself in trouble, he turns to the Eibishter and pours out his heart. When a peasant finds himself with a bottle of wine ..."

"He pours himself a drink," Feivel giggled.

His father smiled, though it was more of a grimace. Each step made his head pound harder — and the pain in his elbow was pure agony. "Don't be afraid, Feivel. Be proud."

"I am," Feivel said.

And it was true. He *was* proud! He'd rather be Feivel, the rabbi's son, even beaten and locked up and held captive, than one of his drunken, boorish captors, however strong they might be. Because, really, they were *not* the strong ones. They didn't have the secret weapon that every Yid possesses. They didn't have a Partner.

Upon reaching the town, they roused the town police chief, who had great respect for the *rav*, and told him about the trio of drunken Poles waiting to be arrested in Jan Stanislaw's farmhouse. Then they woke the doctor, who bandaged the *rav*'s head and neatly popped his dislocated elbow back into place — much to Rabbi Kleinman's relief.

And then they went home.

The moon had set long before, and the eastern sky was beginning to lose its inky blackness. Dawn was not far off. The house was still warm when they finally staggered in. Mrs. Kleinman, who'd been dozing by the dying fire, jerked awake with a start.

She pointed at the stove and mumbled sleepily, "Your dinner's all ready." She yawned. "How late is it? I think I fell asleep ... You took such a long walk. Was it nice?"

Father and son exchanged a smile.

"Very nice, Mother," Feivel replied as he helped his father off with his coat.

Any minute now, his mother would open her eyes properly and see the bandage on her husband's forehead. Any minute now, it would start: the explanations, the stories, the exclamations, the shock.

But right now, in this warm, peaceful haven, Feivel didn't feel like talking. All he wanted was to hang up his father's coat, help him to a chair, and go over to stand by the window.

He wanted to be on hand to see the sun come up, on his first full day as a bar mitzvah.

THE
LEGEND

"**M**a, what's a legend?" Fraidy asked, elbows propped on the kitchen table where she was enjoying an after-school snack.

Mrs. Davidson turned away from the stove to smile at her youngest daughter. "A legend? I suppose it means a story that may or may not be true."

Fraidy frowned. "That doesn't make sense. Esti's not a story."

"Esti?"

"Yes! I was passing through the living room just now, and I heard Esti telling her friend that someone told her she's a legend."

Now it was her mother's turn to frown. "Esti said that?"

"Uh-huh. But I didn't know what 'legend' means."
Fraidy paused. "And I still don't. How can my sister
be a story?"

Slowly, Ma said, "A legend can also mean a person
who's so great that people talk about him — or her —
as something really special ...."

It took Fraidy a moment to work that one out.
"What's so great about Esti?"

The moment the words were out of her mouth, the
little girl had the answer. So did her mother.

Esti's voice. That's what made her great.

Even as a baby, Esti Davidson had seemed born
to sing. She'd been able to imitate sounds exactly on
pitch. As a young child, she'd loved belting out the
songs her nursery and then kindergarten teachers
taught her. But it wasn't until she reached school age
that she really began to shine.

Every choir inevitably featured a solo by Esti. Her
teachers were impressed with her voice, and her Bnos
leaders were awed. Not only was her voice lovely, but
she could also sing any harmony, perfectly on key. And
her voice was powerful enough to fill an auditorium, all
the way to the very last row.

A legend.

Mrs. Davidson went back to the dinner she was
cooking, but her mind was troubled. It was true that Esti
had always received plenty of attention and praise for her
beautiful voice. But a legend? Had she grown so conceit-

ed that she saw herself as somehow larger than life?

Mrs. Davidson was not the only one who was troubled by Esti's view of herself. Every year, the eighth grade at Bais Yaakov put on a small but popular choir for their mothers, grandmothers, sisters, and any other women who wished to attend.

Miriam Newberg, the young woman in charge of this year's choir, loved Esti's voice. It was Esti's attitude that she could have done without ….

"Which solo are you giving me?" Esti demanded, on the very first day of rehearsals.

Familiar with Esti's voice, Miriam hadn't bothered making her try out for the choir. But it irked her that Esti assumed she'd be getting a solo. There were many nice voices among her classmates. Why should she assume anything?

Miriam sighed. Of course Esti would assume she'd get a solo. She always had. Her solos were the highlight of any choir she belonged to.

"I'm not sure yet," Miriam answered. "Let's start learning the songs and I'll let you know."

Esti found her place in the group and waited expectantly for the first practice to begin. She was confident and happy. Choirs were where she felt most at home. Choirs were where she shone.

There were fifteen girls in this choir — fourteen of whom had gone to school with Esti since first grade. The fifteenth girl was named Dina Wallis, and she'd only joined their grade this year. When Dina tried out for a solo, Esti realized something that gave her a little twinge of panic.

Dina Wallis had a beautiful voice.

It was not beautiful in exactly the same way that Esti's was. Where Esti's voice was rich and powerful, Dina's was high and sweet. She sounded like a songbird as she trilled the audition piece. Esti's initial twinge of panic turned into a case of full-blown fear — and jealousy.

She was used to being the undisputed queen of any choir she was in. Was Dina about to steal away her crown?

"So, how was choir practice today?" Mrs. Davidson asked over dinner on the following night.

Esti shrugged. "Not bad. I like the songs we've learned so far. The harmonies are nice, too."

"Will you be singing a solo?"

"Sure! Miriam Newberg, the choir head, gave me a really nice one." As Esti paused, a shadow seemed to cross her face. "She also gave a good solo to the new girl. Dina Wallis."

Fraidy perked up. "Is she a legend, too?"

"No!" Esti glared at her little sister. "I mean, she has a good voice and all that — but a legend? Whatever gave you that idea?"

"Fraidy overheard you telling a friend that *you're* a legend," Ma said with a very pointed look.

Esti had the grace to blush. "Can I help what people say about me?"

"Maybe not," Ma said. "But you *can* help what you repeat."

Legend or not, Esti was not happy about Dina Wallis. Already, girls in her class had begun making admiring noises whenever Dina sang. Esti had received the solo she wanted, but she had a sneaking suspicion that Dina's solo would garner just as much attention as her own. No, Esti wasn't happy at all.

She was about to become a lot unhappier.

"Very nice," Miriam Newberg said after Esti finished singing her solo during the next practice. "But it's missing something ..." She stopped to think for a moment, and then brightened. "I know! It needs some harmony." She looked around. "Dina? Come up here, please."

Dina promptly left her place in line to step up beside Esti at the microphone.

"I want you to sing the high harmony while Esti sings the regular melody," Miriam instructed.

"Hey, that's not fair," Esti protested. "This was supposed to be a solo!"

The minute she said the words, she regretted them. Everyone was looking at her in a pitying way, and some were smirking. The legend was being forced to step aside, to make way for the new queen ….

"This is not about you, or me, or any of us," Miriam said calmly. "It's about making this the best choir it can be. Now, I want to hear how the two of you sound together." She motioned for them to begin.

They sounded glorious together. Esti's strong, true voice blended beautifully with Dina's lighter, sweeter one. The entire choir seemed to hold its breath while the duet was sung.

When it was over, there was a second of utter silence — and then a storm of excited applause.

"That was *awesome!*" someone called out.

"Yes, it was." Miriam was pleased. "That's how we'll do it."

Esti ground her teeth. This was *her* solo! *She* was supposed to stand at center stage under the bright spotlight, basking in the audience's admiration as her voice filled the auditorium and sent shivers down their backs.

Instead, she'd be sharing that spotlight with Dina Wallis.

Instead of basking in the glory of her voice, everyone would be thinking about how nice the two of them sounded together.

Esti would lose that magical feeling of being at the center of attention. She would lose the storm of praise that she loved to hear. She would lose the sense of being somebody special.

She felt as if she was about to lose everything.

Miriam Newberg listened intently as Esti and Dina rehearsed their duet a few days later. Something was wrong.

"There's a problem here," she called up to the stage. "Try it again, girls."

Once again, Esti Davidson and Dina Wallis sang their piece. Miriam frowned. "Esti, you're overpowering Dina. Try to sing more softly."

Esti made a show of "trying," but her next attempt was no different from the first two. Her stronger voice was drowning out Dina's softer one.

"This isn't working," Miriam said, almost to herself.

But Esti heard. And she smiled.

With a start, Miriam realized that Esti didn't *want* it to work. She didn't want to sing a duet with Dina. She wanted the spotlight all to herself.

Walking home later, Miriam tried to figure out what to do. Her first reaction was to be furious with Esti. How dare she try to sabotage a lovely duet like that? Was she so stuck-up that she couldn't bear the thought of Dina Wallis enjoying some admiration as well?

Or maybe not …

Miriam recalled the look in Esti's eyes when she'd announced that she was turning Esti's solo into a duet. There had been something in her expression … almost as if she were afraid.

Afraid of what?

Miriam tried to imagine what it was like to grow up as … well, as a legend. Esti had never had to share the spotlight with anyone before. Her voice had always carried the day.

But, except for her stunning voice, she was just like everybody else. Her voice was the one thing that made her feel special. Those moments of wild admiration when she sang were like bread and water to her. They fed her. They kept her alive … or at least Esti believed they did. Now Esti was like a person who was afraid she'd starve to death if someone took away the food that she needed to live.

Esti Davidson was not really stuck-up. In fact, just the opposite was true. She was scared of losing the one thing that made her feel special. Because, without it, she believed she was nothing at all …

Miriam had been planning to give Esti a stern talking-to. Now she understood why the girl was trying to push her rival out of the spotlight. She was terrified of losing her place in the world.

The question was: What was Miriam going to do about it?

Though Miriam secretly hoped that the situation would somehow clear up on its own, the next practice made it all too clear that the problem was not about to go away. Each time Esti and Dina stood up to sing their piece together, Esti's voice completely drowned out Dina's. Esti was making no real attempt to change that. She was using her voice to nudge Dina away from "her" solo — and "her" spotlight.

It was time for Plan B.

By some deft maneuvering, Miriam made sure she was walking just in front of Esti as the girls trooped down the school corridor on their way out of the building after the next night's rehearsal. Suddenly, Miriam stopped short. She slapped her jacket pocket and then began frantically searching the ground at her feet.

Esti noticed something dark on the floor and bent to pick it up. It was a wallet.

"Is this yours?" Esti asked, hurrying up to the choir head with the wallet in her hand.

Miriam's face registered relief. "Yes! Where did you find it?"

"It was right here on the floor. It must've fallen out of your pocket just now."

"That'll teach me to leave my wallet in my pocket like that." Miriam tucked the wallet into her purse and started walking again, motioning for Esti to fall into step beside her. The other choir girls passed them by, some throwing them curious glances as they went.

"So, tell me," Miriam said. "Were you tempted?"

Esti was confused. "Tempted? To do what?"

"To keep my wallet, of course."

"*What*?" Esti stopped walking. "Of course not! How could you even *think* such a thing? I would *never* steal someone's wallet!"

"Why not?"

"Because ... because ..." Esti stopped and took a deep breath. "Because it's wrong!"

Miriam was relentless. "*Why* is it wrong?"

Esti peered at the older girl suspiciously. "It's wrong because Hashem said so!"

"You mean," Miriam said, "because Hashem decided to give this wallet and this money to me, and not to you?"

"Uh, something like that ..."

"Just like He decided to give Dina Wallis a beautiful voice that people may admire as much as they admire yours?"

Esti's mouth opened and closed without making a sound.

By this time, the corridor was deserted. The rest of the choir was outside, either walking home in groups or waiting to be picked up by parents. In a minute, Miriam would have to let Esti go. But not before she tried to drive home her all-important point.

"Hashem gives everyone exactly what he or she is supposed to have," she said softly. "Whether it's money, beauty, health ... or talent. Right?"

Mutely, Esti nodded. Her eyes were very big.

"So, if Dina Wallis has a nice voice, and if that

voice wins her some praise and attention in our choir, that must mean that Hashem decided to give her those gifts. Right?"

Another nod. Esti blinked back some tears. Miriam's heart twisted in compassion.

"For years and years, Hashem gave you gifts, Esti," she said earnestly. "And He's still giving them to you. He's just asking you to share a little. Do you think you can do that?"

Esti looked down. With a sniffle, she said honestly, "I-I'm not sure. It's hard …."

"I know. But it's the right thing to do. Just like returning my wallet was the right thing."

Miriam waited.

Her patience was rewarded at last. Esti looked back up at her and tried to smile. "I must seem like such a baby. But …"

"It's hard. I know it is. But will you do it?" Miriam asked again.

Esti nodded. "I'll try my best." She was about to walk on.

"One more thing, Esti."

Esti turned to look at the choir head curiously.

"There are lots of ways to be special. Having a talent is just one of them," Miriam said. "Another way is being such a wonderful person that everyone looks up to you and learns from you."

"Who, me? I could *never* be that way."

"Sure, you can! In fact, you just started — by deciding to control your *yetzer hara* and try not to be jealous of Dina. See?"

A honk sounded from beyond the glass doors that led to the street. Esti's father was waiting to drive her home.

"Thanks a lot," Esti said shyly.

"Don't mention it," Miriam replied. "I expect to hear great things from you one day, Esti. And I don't mean just your singing voice."

"I'll try ..."

"I'm sure you'll succeed. Who knows?" Miriam grinned broadly. "If you work *really* hard, one day you just may become ... a legend!"

Esti didn't know about that. But as she stood beside Dina Wallis on the night of their performance, and heard their voices float out into the darkened auditorium like twin birds flying in perfect harmony, she did know something else.

She knew, in the deepest way, that peace is better than rivalry, and sharing is better than pushing away.

And from the way the rapt audience was drinking in their song, she knew that every single one of them knew it, too.

HOME
RUN

There I was, exactly the way I'd pictured it in a million daydreams.

Two strong kids were carrying me on their shoulders while a dozen or so others crowded around, looking up at me and cheering at the top of their voices. The sun baked my back as those cheers filled my ears. When I looked down, all I could see was a sea of boys, red-faced in the sun. Boys with *tzitzis* flying as they pumped their fists in the air. Boys wearing their biggest smiles — and cheering.

Cheering for *me*!

I held on tight to the shoulders that were holding me up, and let the sound of those cheers fill me up from my toes to my eyebrows. The whole world seemed to be one enormous voice, yelling, *"Shi-mi! Shi-mi!"*

They were shouting for me.

I rode those shoulders, floating ten feet high in the air. I listened to them chant my name. I looked out over the sweating, grinning, cheering crowd like a king surveying his kingdom.

And all I could think was: *I don't belong here.*

It was a funny thing to think, since this was the moment I'd been dreaming about for such a long time.

Back when I was really little, in first grade, I was what you'd call a nerdy kind of kid. On the quiet side. A little shy. The kind of kid who has a hard time holding back tears when someone splashes him in the pool. School seemed very big and scary. I had my hands full just trying to figure out what was going on and keeping up with everything.

Then, in fourth grade, I went through what my mother called a growth spurt. Suddenly, I was taller than most of the kids in my class. Until then, I'd avoided the games that other kids played in the school yard. I was scared I'd get hit with a ball or something. But now, I decided to try. There wasn't much else to do during recess except play ball anyway. So I took my chances — and was pleasantly surprised to find that I could do it. When it came to team sports, I could hold my own.

As time went on, I could more than hold my own. At recess, the captains started choosing me for their teams instead of leaving me for last. I started spending Sunday afternoons and the long springtime evenings playing stickball in the empty lot at the end of our block. Stickball gave way to baseball, with some basketball thrown in when there weren't enough guys around for two good baseball teams.

And all along, I had this picture in my mind.

It was a secret picture. I didn't tell anyone about it, not even Ma, though I told her most things. A lot of kids I know have mothers who don't talk much about anything, except to tell them to wear a coat when it's cold, and eat breakfast, and go to bed on time. My mother's different. I can talk to her about stuff — important stuff — and she listens. When I have a problem, she gives me pretty good advice. I'm lucky, I guess.

But I didn't tell Ma about the picture in my head, because it's a boy thing. I wasn't sure if she'd understand.

One thing she definitely didn't understand was the kids I hung around with. I don't know if it's the same at your school, but in mine, the kids who are the best ballplayers are the kings of the class. Everyone looks up to them. Everyone wants to *be* them. I sure wanted to.

Don't tell anyone … but even as I was acing those ball games, inside I was still that shy little kid trying not to cry in the pool. Know what I mean? I was a lot taller now, and a lot better at all the things I used to find so hard. But part of me didn't know that. Part of me still felt small and scared.

And that part needed to attach myself to kids who were big and unafraid. The kind of kids who were team captains instead of waiting around on the sidelines, hoping to be picked.

So I made friends with those kids. We hung out together, played a lot of ball, and shared a lot of laughs. When they came over to my house, they made a lot of noise and left the playroom looking as if a hurricane had hit it. Luckily, most of the time they left the playroom alone because I had a hoop in my backyard that they liked much better.

Ma didn't enjoy having them around. She didn't exactly come out and say so, but I could tell. Once, she asked me, "What do you *see* in those boys, Shimi?" I just shrugged.

But I knew exactly what I saw in them. I saw in them the person I wished I could be.

When some of my friends signed up for a certain camp, I decided to sign up, too. It took some convincing. My parents had been thinking of a different place. But, in the end, they agreed to let me go.

All camps have sports, but in this camp they

make a really big deal about them. After the first week or two, we were divided into teams — and then, the competition *really* started! All we could talk about at breakfast, lunch, or supper was which team was leading and which ones were falling behind. We were working our way up to the playoffs, when the two top teams would play each other. It was the highlight of the whole summer.

With the playoffs coming up, we were playing hard. There were just two teams doing better than us. And then, after a great game, in which I hit a double in the fourth inning and a triple in the eighth, we moved up to second place. At supper that night, the head counselor made the announcement we'd all been waiting for. Our team had made it. We were in the playoffs!

The big game took place on a really hot day, the kind that makes you want to sit quietly in the shade and drink something cold. But we were nowhere near the shade. We were out on the ball field, and the whole camp had come to watch us play.

From the start, you could see that the two teams were evenly matched. First our team was up one run, and then the other team was. We couldn't seem to shake them off. I was giving it my best, and I know that everyone else on my team was doing the same. The trouble was, the other team was just as good. As the innings went by, I started feeling really tense. By the ninth inning I was a bundle of nerves.

The other team went first, and scored twice. They were leading us by two runs. Then it was our turn at bat. We'd have to score at least three runs to beat them. My heart was thumping so hard, I could hardly breathe. It seemed to be stuck right in my throat. The first batter on our side struck out. So did the second.

But the next three batters all hit singles! There was still hope. Two outs, three men on base.

And then it was my turn up at bat.

I don't know if you've ever been under that kind of pressure before. Believe me, you don't want to be. My play was going to make or break the game for our side.

I tried not to think of that as I stepped up to the plate. I tried not to think about anything. Mostly, I was just trying to breathe. So much adrenalin was pumping through me that the bat felt like a twig in my hand. I hefted it a few times, getting the feel of it. Then I put it to my shoulder.

"Strike one!" I never hated anything as much as I hated the ump's voice at that minute.

The ball came at me again. I swung hard.

"Strike two!"

Something surged through me, something that felt like anger, something so focused that the whole world shrank down to just two things: that ball and me. I fixed my eye on the ball as the pitcher aimed, and I kept my eye on it as it hurled through the air in my direction. The bat felt like a part of me, a third arm. I swung with all my might — and connected.

Every muscle I owned went into that swing. I ripped into that ball with a power I didn't know I had. And that ball went flying!

"*Run!*" my teammates screamed. "Run, Shimi!"

Boy, *did* I ever run! The power that had been in my arms when I swung that bat moved down into my legs. I raced to first base like the wind, pounded into second like a cannonball, and sprinted over to third like a bullet. And all that time, the ball kept flying.

People started to yell.

"It's over the fence!"

"It's gone!"

"It's a HOME RUN!"

Gasping for breath, I jogged over to home plate.

That's when the cheers erupted, and strong arms grabbed me and threw me onto stronger shoulders. That's when the picture I'd been carrying around in my head for so long finally came true.

They paraded me around that field like I was the hero of the world. They were cheering me, and calling my name, and gazing up at me like they'd never seen me before and didn't want to look at anyone else ever again.

And it was right then, as I was riding on top of the world, that I had that funny thought:

I don't belong here.

Like I said, I have the kind of mother you can talk to. And I really felt like I needed to talk to her then. The playoff game was on a Thursday, and Friday afternoon I was standing in line with a bunch of other kids, waiting to use the phones to call home.

"Hi, Ma," I said, when my turn finally came.

"Hi, Shimi. What's new in camp?"

"Oh, nothing much … We had a big playoff game yesterday. I hit the winning home run."

"That's wonderful, Shimi! That must have made you happy."

"Sure …" I hesitated. "Ma? Are you still coming on Tuesday?" That would be the day between the two halves of the summer.

"Of course! We'll drive over from the bungalow colony … Is something wrong?" Ma can always tell what I'm feeling.

"No … not really. Just something I wanted to talk to you about."

"Can you talk now?"

I looked around at the zillions of kids talking on the phones or waiting to use them, and shook my head. "Not really. But maybe we can find a little time on Tuesday?"

Tuesday morning turned out to be much cooler. The sky was gray and full of rain that refused to fall. I was glad to see my family when they drove up in our good old minivan.

For a while, we all hung out together. And then, with a sideways look at me, Ma suggested that my father take my younger brothers over to the lake to feed the ducks. Ma and I waited until they were out of sight, and then started walking in the other direction.

"So, what's the problem, Shimi? You seem to be having a great summer here."

"I am."

"But ...?" Ma prompted.

I took a deep breath. "Remember that home run I hit in the playoffs?"

She nodded.

"You should've seen me, Ma. Everyone was carrying me around on their shoulders, and cheering and everything. But I kept thinking ... it wasn't really *me*. It was like I was acting a part in a play or something." I stopped and looked at my mother to see if she understood.

Ma nodded thoughtfully. "You're getting older, Shimi. You'll be a bar mitzvah soon. Maybe you suddenly realized that there's more to life than playing ball."

I considered this. "I still like playing ball, Ma. What bothered me was hearing them cheer for me like that, just because I got a home run."

"What was the problem, exactly?"

I hesitated, and then burst out, "It wasn't *me* they were cheering for. They were cheering for the batter who'd hit the ball out of the field. Not *me*."

Ma waited, a little puzzled. I tried to explain. "I always had this picture in my head, you know? A picture of myself hitting a home run and winning an important game. And then, last week, it happened! For a few minutes, it felt awesome."

"And then …?"

I shrugged. "Then it stopped feeling so good. If people are going to admire me, I want it to be because I did something *really* great. Because *I'm* great. Not because I just hit a ball hard enough to help us win a game."

Ma was quiet for a while, thinking over what I'd just told her. Then she said, "Maybe you're ready for a different role model now, Shimi."

"A different what?"

"Role model. For a long time now, your head has been filled with baseball, and wanting to be like the kids who are good at sports. Maybe it's time to look around again and figure out what kind of people you *really* admire. And then try to be like them."

I looked at her. "You mean, here in camp?"

"That's a good place to start. Is there anyone here who you look up to?"

My counselor's a pretty good guy. Ditto for the

head counselor and a couple of other awesome guys. But the first two people who popped into my head when Ma asked that question were in my own bunk.

"There's Menachem," I said slowly.

"Menachem?"

"He's a kid in my bunk who always seems to disappear at rest hour. Finally, I asked him where he goes."

"And?"

"And he said ... the infirmary. He said there's usually at least one or two kids in there who have a virus or fever or something, and they can't play or be with their friends. So he goes and sits with them, just to keep them company and cheer them up."

"I see." Ma smiled. "Sounds like Menachem has a kind heart."

I nodded. "For sure ... And there's also this other kid. His name's Binyamin. In the morning, when we learn, most of the other boys are just counting the minutes till they can run out and play. But not Binyamin. He's really into it, you know? He asks Rebbi lots of questions, and sometimes he gives really good answers to Rebbi's questions."

"And you admire that?"

"I sure do. Boy, does that kid have brains!"

"It's not just brains, you know. It sounds like Binyamin really *wants* to learn. He's interested."

"Unlike me, you mean?"

"Unlike a lot of kids, from what you've been telling me."

We walked along the path, dodging little kids and smiling politely at their parents. A few other families had come up for the day, too. I was quiet, thinking about Menachem and Binyamin, and comparing them to the kids I'd been hanging around these past couple of years.

Maybe it *was* time for a change.

The picture I'd been dreaming about for so long had finally come true. And it made me happy ... for a couple of minutes. But the happiness went away. When kids came over to me for hours afterwards, congratulating me on that home run, I felt like an imposter. Yes, I hit that ball. But no, I didn't really deserve the hero-worship I saw in their eyes.

I didn't really deserve anything. Because I still hadn't *done* anything yet. Nothing important, I mean.

Maybe later, when my family went home, I'd spend some quality time with Menachem. And when I didn't really understand the Gemara, I'd go over to Binyamin and ask him to explain it to me. Maybe the two of them could help me figure out a different kind of picture to carry around in my head from now on.

Because the next time I was riding high, I wanted it to be for something *real*. I wanted to earn the kind of cheers you can't hear with your ears.

It's great to hit a ball out of the field — but when

the game's over, all you have is a memory and a lost ball. From now on, I wanted to pour my energy into something that lasts. Something that keeps growing.

Something real.

I wanted to hit the kind of home run that counts — and see my name in lights, on a scoreboard that *really* matters ….

I gave my mother a big smile. If we hadn't been in the middle of camp with lots of people around, I probably would've given her a big hug, too. "Thanks," I said.

And even though I didn't say a word about my plans, I could tell that she knew. Like I said, Ma understands.

But all she said was, "You're very welcome, Shimi."

And then we turned around and started for the lake, to help Ta and my brothers feed the ducks.

AVIGAYIL'S SECRET

Every morning, Avigayil met Batsheva on the corner, after which they walked to school together.

Avigayil almost always got there first. Mornings were her best time of the day. She had no trouble jumping out of bed even before her alarm clock rang, ready to face the day.

Batsheva, on the other hand, was a night owl. No matter how many girls might be walking down the block, it was never hard for Avigayil to spot her friend. Batsheva was the one who wore a sleepy scowl and moved as if the weight of the world was on her shoulders. It wasn't until about midday that Batsheva really started to wake up, and she was at her liveliest when the bell rang at the end of the school day.

Avigayil reached their corner a little earlier than usual that Monday morning. She settled in for a long wait. Batsheva always said that Monday was her worst day. That was because she tended to stay up even later than usual over the weekend, which made the process of waking up on Mondays sheer torture.

But Avigayil didn't mind the wait. She was feeling good that morning. She wore a smile that seemed to embrace the houses, the trees … the whole world. It embraced Batsheva, too, when that girl finally put in an appearance wearing her mopey morning face.

"What are *you* so happy about?" she grumped as she joined her friend. "You're not *allowed* to be happy on a Monday morning!"

"Sorry," Avigayil said, smiling even more. "I forgot." She seemed to be hugging a secret joy to herself.

This made Batsheva curious — so curious that she even forgot how tired she was as they turned and began walking in the direction of school. "Really, Avigayil, what's going on? Did something good happen today?"

Avigayil's mouth crinkled into a quiet grin. "You could say that …."

"Well, what is it? Tell me."

"It's nothing." Avigayil picked up her pace slightly, as though she wanted to move away from the topic.

"So you're happy about 'nothing'?"

"I meant … I don't want to talk about it. It's kind of private."

Batsheva's curiosity, which had been flickering like a tiny flame before, was in full blaze now. She was a girl who liked to be in the know. There was nothing that challenged Batsheva more than a secret. She liked solving mysteries, and here was one that concerned her best friend. She pressed harder.

"Is it so private that you can't share it with your best friend in the whole world?"

Avigayil sighed. "Bats, you know that I tell you most things. But some things I just prefer to keep to myself. All right?"

It was *not* all right with Batsheva — but she decided to bide her time. She'd try again later, when Avigayil wasn't expecting it. If there was one thing Batsheva had, it was persistence.

Sooner or later, her friend would crack.

The ten minutes before the first bell rang were filled with the moans and groans of girls who hadn't gotten enough sleep the night before. Most of Avigayil's classmates seemed to be proud to stay awake into the wee hours, just like Batsheva. None of them could relate to Avigayil's love of mornings — which was why she kept quiet about it. Especially on Monday mornings, when the class's night owls were particularly miserable.

Batsheva waited until lunchtime, when they were settled at a table with their sandwiches, before bringing up the topic again.

"I'm still curious, Avigayil. What happened to make you so cheerful this morning?"

"I'm always cheerful in the morning," her friend replied evasively.

"But you were especially happy *this* morning. You even admitted that something good had happened. So tell me already!"

"Batsheva, it's nothing to talk about. Nothing really 'happened.'"

"But you said it did!"

Avigayil was starting to feel annoyed. "Can't a person keep anything to herself? Do I have to tell you everything?"

Batsheva looked hurt. "I thought we were best friends …."

"We are! I'd just rather not talk about this. Okay?"

Batsheva frowned. She was not about to give up until she learned her friend's secret. But Avigayil was looking stubborn, so she managed to hold her tongue.

Later, she promised herself.

Avigayil could have predicted what would happen on the walk home from school. If Batsheva had been persistent this morning, when she was barely awake, she would be as eager as a bloodhound later in the day.

She wasn't wrong.

"This is so unfair," Batsheva complained as they trudged along, backpacks on their shoulders. "I tell you all *my* secrets. Why won't you tell me yours?"

Avigayil managed to hold onto her temper. "Bats, I told you — it's no big deal. This has nothing to do with you."

"Then why won't you tell me?"

"Because it's my business and not yours!"

The minute she said those words, Avigayil regretted them. Now Batsheva would be hurt, and Avigayil didn't want that. She just wanted her friend to drop the subject already. Batsheva *was* hurt by her friend's tone — but her curiosity was even stronger. Swallowing her pride, she wheedled, "Even if it's none of my business, can't you tell me anyway?"

Luckily for Avigayil, a couple of other classmates caught up with them at that point, and they all walked on together. Nothing more was said about Avigayil's secret.

Avigayil said good-bye at her door and turned her back on the others with a quiet sigh of relief.

But bloodhounds are persistent, and so was Batsheva. The phone rang right after supper that night.

"Avigayil!" her mother called. "It's for you!"

The minute she heard her friend's voice, Avigayil's heart sank. It was not unusual for Batsheva to call her in the evenings. In fact, it happened nearly every night. But Avigayil was in no mood for what she was certain was coming.

"You know," Batsheva began, "I was thinking."

"Congratulations," Avigayil said dryly.

Batsheva chuckled. "No, seriously. I was thinking about trust. Of all the things that make a friendship strong, don't you think that trust is the most important?"

"Trust is important," Avigayil agreed cautiously.

"Then why won't you trust *me*? I know how to keep a secret!"

"This is not that kind of secret." Avigayil's patience was wearing thin. "It's just … personal. So just drop it, okay?"

Batsheva moved into dramatic mode. "My — own — best — friend!" she declaimed mournfully. "My very best friend in the whole wide world has a secret — and she won't tell me!"

"Drop it, Batsheva. I told you, this has nothing to do with you."

"My own best friend says that her life has nothing to do with me," Batsheva announced in a voice of deepest gloom. "I'm so disappointed. I'm so disillusioned. I'm so —"

"Curious," Avigayil finished for her, with a sigh.

"Yes! *So tell me the secret!*"

"G'nite, Bats." Avigayil gently hung up the phone.

Avigayil got ready for bed early that night — so early that when Batsheva called again, she was told that Avigayil was unavailable. This made Batsheva wonder if her friend was angry at her for trying to ferret out the secret. All this wondering kept her up even later than usual, making her especially droopy the next morning.

Avigayil was waiting at the corner, as always. The two girls eyed each other uneasily. Avigayil braced herself for the next onslaught.

Batsheva noticed. She saw her best friend steel herself against the curiosity that had impelled her to nag Avigayil endlessly the day before. And still, she had to ask …

"Changed your mind, Avigayil? Maybe you want to share the secret with me now?"

Avigayil just looked at the ground and shrugged.

All at once, Batsheva was mad. Burning mad. She started walking very fast, not even bothering to see if Avigayil was keeping up with her.

For the rest of the day, the two girls did not exchange another word.

Avigayil was unhappy. Batsheva had been avoiding her all day. As she packed up her backpack late that afternoon, she sneaked a peek at Batsheva — who was looking at anyone but her.

What am I doing? Avigayil thought suddenly. Was her so-called "secret" worth making her best friend angry at her?

She took a deep breath and approached Batsheva.

"Sorry about this morning," she said in a breathless rush. "If you'll walk home with me, I'll ... I'll tell you what you want to know."

Batsheva perked up instantly. "Great! Let's go."

The two girls walked out of the building into the late-afternoon sun. It was a warm day, with just a hint of spring in the air. A day when you wanted to be on good terms with everyone and everything. Avigayil matched her steps to her friend's as they put the school behind them.

"Well?" Batsheva prompted eagerly.

Avigayil closed her eyes for a minute. This wouldn't be easy to talk about. She wished she didn't have to. But Batsheva's friendship was worth more than her discomfort.

She marshaled her thoughts, then looked at her friend. "Okay," she said slowly. "Here goes ..."

Suddenly, Batsheva thought, *What am I doing?*

It was clear as daylight that Avigayil would rather not talk about this. She was doing so only because

Batsheva had been distant and angry with her all day.

Is this any way to treat a friend? Forcing her to do something she doesn't want to do — just because I happen to be curious? What kind of friend does that make me?

"Yesterday morning …," Avigayil began.

"Don't," Batsheva said quickly, before she could go on.

Avigayil blinked. "What?"

"Don't tell me. I can see that you don't want to. I — I'd rather you keep it to yourself, if that'll make you more comfortable."

And suddenly, because Batsheva cared enough about her to say that, Avigayil found that she wanted to tell her.

"That's okay," she said. "I don't mind."

"But I do!" Batsheva insisted. "Don't tell me, Avigayil."

"But I *want* to tell you!"

"Well, I don't want to hear it!"

Startled, the two girls met each other's eyes. Then they started to laugh.

"Listen to us," Avigayil giggled. "Don't we sound silly?"

"*I* was silly yesterday," Batsheva said. "I shouldn't have pushed you so hard when you didn't want to tell."

"Maybe not. But maybe I was too stubborn about not telling."

The pair walked down the block in companionable silence.

"Bats?"

"Hmm?"

"Can I tell you my secret? Pretty please?"

Batsheva slanted a look at her. "Are you sure you want to?"

"Positive ..."

On Wednesday morning, the sun rose red and glorious above the trees and the rooftops. And Avigayil was there to see it.

In fact, this was the third morning in a row that she'd been up to greet the sun.

As sometimes occurred, she'd found herself awake extra early on Monday morning, and decided to get out of bed instead of turning over for a little more sleep. And because of what happened next, she'd woken up extra early again yesterday and today — on purpose.

On Monday morning, Avigayil had taken her *siddur* and davened the morning *brachos* together with the sunrise.

Never in her life had davening been so meaningful. As she'd faced the rising sun and remembered its Creator, her heart had been filled to overflowing with deep, beautiful thoughts. Thoughts that she'd never had before. Thoughts that she didn't want to share with anybody. This was strictly between her and Hashem.

But as she closed her *siddur* and kissed it on Wednesday morning, after her third sunrise davening, she recalled how she'd tried to share the experience with her best friend yesterday. It hadn't been easy to find the words. But, somehow, Batsheva had understood.

Batsheva, the night owl, was not likely to experience the beauty of early-morning *tefillah* that Avigayil had just discovered. But she *could* share the feeling secondhand — through her best friend.

A secret that's dragged out of you against your will, Avigayil thought dreamily, *can leave a scar. But a secret willingly shared is something else entirely …*

She kissed her *siddur* again and went to the kitchen for some breakfast. Soon she'd be standing at their corner, waiting for Batsheva to come trudging half asleep up the block to meet her.

This time, her friend wouldn't ask what she was so happy about, in a growling voice that said she couldn't imagine what possible reason a person could have for smiling in the morning.

Because now, she knew.

THE
BIG TEST

A t first there were only two of us: Fraydie and me. After we'd been friends for a few months, Shevi sort of drifted in. We stayed like that for a while, three close friends who did practically everything together.

And then, one Sunday afternoon at a school carnival, Debby and Minna ended up spending a lot of time with us. When the carnival was over, we all went back to my house, where a great time was had by all. After that, the two of them were officially part of our circle. We had become a fivesome.

Actually, it was Debby who became our friend. Minna lived on Debby's block, and since she was also in our class at school it was only natural that the two of them were friendly. But the moment Debby joined our group, she seemed much more our friend than Minna's.

Minna was on the quiet side — nice enough, but without the sparkle and sense of fun that make girls popular in middle school. We included her in our plans because she seemed to want to be part of them — but if she hadn't been there we probably wouldn't have noticed, or cared. Minna was like the furniture in a room: You don't have any problem with it being there, but you don't seek it out. You don't spend much time playing with the sofa, or having a conversation with a dining room chair ....

In this way, we muddled through the second half of seventh grade and finally started the eighth. There were lots of exciting things to keep us busy that year: the play, the yearbook, and the distant goal of graduation. But the biggest thing that loomed before us was getting accepted into the high school of our choice.

Naturally, all five of us wanted to be together. We lived in a neighborhood that had several good options. It was Minna who said that she was applying to Bais Shprintza. Eventually, all of our parents decided on that school for us. Applications were filled out, and the date of the entrance test was announced. On an afternoon just three weeks away, the five of us — along with plenty of other girls — would sit down to take the test that would decide whether or not we were accepted.

I was nervous. Correction: I was *very* nervous. I'm not the world's most studious girl, though when I try I usually get decent, if not dazzling, marks. And I was trying now. I studied whenever I had a free minute, trying to anticipate the kinds of questions that would be asked. By the time we'd reached the home stretch — the last few days before the big test — I was worn out with studying. I wanted to spend the last Shabbos before the test simply relaxing. I invited all my friends to come to my house on Shabbos afternoon.

For one reason or another, my friends never made it to my house that day. Later, I found out what those reasons were. Fraydie's cousins came over, so she had to stay home and entertain them. Shevi had come down with a cold and didn't want to venture out because the day was chilly and overcast. Debby had been up very late the night before, reading a good book, and she decided to rest at home that afternoon and try to finish it. I waited and waited, but for a long time no one came knocking at my door.

And then — at long last — there was a knock. Eagerly, I ran to open the door. There stood Minna, all by herself.

It's a strange thing, but up until that day I'd never really been alone with Minna. Whenever I saw her, it was together with at least one of our other friends. We stood staring at each other, she on the doorstep and I with my hand on the doorknob and a look of eager expectation on my face. As my brain registered that she was alone, and that I'd have to spend the afternoon with no one but quiet, not-very-exciting Minna, I could feel my expectant look start to fade. In a minute, my grin of welcome would turn into a grimace of disappointment … if I let it.

I took a deep breath and turned the corners of my mouth up instead. "Minna!" I exclaimed, trying to make my voice sound happy instead of just surprised. "Come in!"

"I stopped at Debby's house to pick her up," Minna explained as she walked hesitantly inside, "but she's really tired and decided to stay home and rest." She looked around. "Where is everyone?"

"Believe it or not, you're the only one who showed up!" I said merrily, though my heart quailed at the thought of the next few hours. "And I bought enough nosh for an army! C'mon, let's get started."

Minna smiled, though there was a look in her eye that was as uncomfortable as the way I was feeling. "Thanks, Elky …." She followed me into the kitchen.

After making desultory conversation over chips and pretzels, I invited her to play a game of checkers. "I had a checkers tournament with my cousin when we were at her house for *yom tov*," I said, getting out the board. "I've developed some strategies that I'd love to try out on you."

"You'll beat me, for sure," Minna said, with another bashful smile. "I'm not very good at checkers."

"So I'll teach you. C'mon!" Playing the hearty hostess was exhausting, but I tried not to show it. If my other friends had been there, we'd have been talking a mile a minute and laughing our heads off every other second. Anything we played would have been fun. I was not especially looking forward to playing checkers with Minna, but she was here and I didn't want her to feel bad about coming.

I won our first game so easily that Minna almost refused to play another. But I taught her some tricks, and we tried again. This time, she played a little better. The minutes ticked by. After four games and another round of nosh, I thought it might be time for Minna to start thinking about heading home. Then a swishing sound at the window made me realize that it had started to rain.

"I guess you'd better stay for *shalosh seudos*," I said, with a cheerfulness I was far from feeling. Then, because I was afraid she might have heard a false note in my voice, I redoubled the invitation. "Please stay, Minna."

She looked uncertainly from me to the window, and back again. "It's not raining so hard," she said doubtfully. "If I walk fast, I won't get too wet ...."

"You're staying," I said firmly. "C'mon, Minna. It'll be fun!"

Fun was the last thing I expected the next couple of hours to bring, but what choice was there? Minna was my guest, and my parents had always taught us that guests have to be treated like royalty. So we played some more checkers — Minna actually became quite good at it by the time the day was over — and then my family and Minna sat down to the third Shabbos meal. My little sister took a liking to her and begged her to read some storybooks, which carried us all the way through to Havdalah. And then Shabbos was over, and Minna called her father, asking to be picked up.

As we waited for him, Minna turned shyly to me. "I had a really nice time, Elky. Thanks for having me."

"What's to thank?" I said heartily. "Besides, you've been here a million times before."

"But never by myself," she said simply. "It must have been a little boring for you …."

"What are you talking about? It was fun! You're becoming a great checkers player, Minna!"

She smiled but said nothing. We heard a honk outside. With a quick "thank you" to my mother and a "see you" to me, she was gone.

I closed the door behind her, heaving a big sigh of relief. It hadn't been easy, acting so cheerful and hearty for so long. I hoped it had worked. I hoped Minna had felt comfortable.

And then I put the whole thing out of my mind and went to call my friends, to find out why none of them had bothered to show up that afternoon.

It was the day of the big test. I couldn't remember ever being so nervous before. As I stared down at the test paper in front of me, my mind went blank. By the time my thoughts started moving again, I'd lost some valuable minutes. I hurried to get started, hoping that all the material I'd studied would come back when I needed it ….

And then the test was over — and the waiting began.

We'd been told not to expect an answer for at least two weeks. Those were a strange couple of weeks. On the surface, we went about our normal lives: school, homework, lazy Shabbos afternoons, evenings filled with endless phone calls. But underneath it all, we were waiting. And worrying. At least, *I* was worrying. A lot.

My friends seemed pretty confident that they'd done okay on the test. As for me, I wasn't so sure. The waiting was like a long, drawn-out torture.

And then, Debby got her letter. She'd been accepted!

Over the course of the next few days, Fraydie and Shevi and Minna got their acceptance letters, too.

Which left me, biting my nails and wondering if there had been a clerical oversight ... or if I'd actually been rejected by Bais Shprintza.

I tried to put on a good act with my friends, but I'm sure they saw right through me.

"The letter was probably lost in the mail," Fraydie said. "Have your mother call them, Elky!"

"No," I said sadly. "I may as well face it. I didn't get in."

Shevi and Debby made similar, encouraging remarks. Minna just looked at me, saying nothing, but her eyes were full of sympathy.

The next few days were a nightmare. I tried to picture a future that didn't include my circle of best friends — and failed utterly. I could hardly even picture myself in high school, let alone in a school where I wasn't close to anyone. I talked to my parents, trying to figure out where else to apply. At night, when no one could see me, I cried buckets of tears into my pillow.

It was a nightmare.

And then I came home from school one day, and my mother practically ran to meet me at the door. She was waving an envelope. "The letter came, Elky!" she cried. "Look!"

I looked at the envelope in my mother's hand. It

was addressed to my parents, but it was about me. It said, in black and white, that they were happy to inform my parents that their daughter, Elky, had been accepted into the ninth grade at Bais Shprintza!

I was never so happy in my life. After hugging my mother tightly and receiving her congratulatory kiss in return, I raced upstairs to call my friends. We would be together next year after all! I was in!

The year finally ended, and the summer passed. And then it was time to start our new lives as high school girls. I was thrilled to put on my new school uniform and set off for Bais Shprintza on that clear September morning: the first day of school.

The morning passed in a blur of new faces, new names, new goals. When lunchtime came, we sat over our sandwiches, comparing notes. A girl sauntered over to our table.

"Which one of you is Minna Halpert?"

Minna pointed at herself and looked up at the girl questioningly.

"I heard you're the principal's niece."

Minna blushed. "Uh … great-niece, actually."

The girl grinned. "Hey, put in a good word for me, okay?"

"S-sure." Minna tried to smile, too. As the girl walked away, we all turned to Minna.

"How come you didn't tell us that Rebbetzin Furman is your great-aunt?" Shevi demanded.

Minna shrugged. "I didn't think it was important to mention it."

"Well, it'll be a little weird for you, won't it? Being related to the principal, I mean."

"Maybe." Minna hesitated. "But sometimes, it's also useful ..." She peeked over at me.

I don't think she meant for me to see that glance. But I did — and I started to wonder.

My late acceptance ... Minna's sympathy ... the principal of Bais Shprintza ... Minna's great-aunt ...

Suddenly, I thought about that Shabbos afternoon earlier in the year, when I'd tried my best to be a gracious hostess and to make Minna feel wanted, even though I hadn't felt very gracious or welcoming inside.

Two tests.

Luckily, I'd passed one of them. And that had brought me the best reward of all.

I looked across the lunch table at Minna, and the smile I gave her was full of all the things I couldn't say.

But the smile she sent back told me that she heard them anyway — loud and clear.

YUDI
OVERSLEPT

One overcast Monday in July, Yudi Stein woke up groggily after a night that felt far too short. It was his own fault: He'd stayed up late the night before, playing an endless game of Monopoly with his sisters. That wasn't a problem for the girls; *they* didn't have to get up for *minyan* in the morning.

He turned over in bed. His pillow felt softer than usual, and the quiet hum of the air-conditioning reminded him of how hot it would probably be outside today. Of course, he'd have to go out anyway, to make it to day camp on time ... What time *was* it? He cracked open an eye to check the clock by his bed.

Both eyes flew open. He'd overslept! He was supposed to be up twenty minutes ago. He must have slept right through his alarm. Or maybe he'd forgotten to set it last night … In any case, he was going to be really late for his usual *minyan.*

Or maybe not? If he leaped out of bed this instant, washed his hands and threw on his clothes in a fraction of the time it usually took him, and then ran like the wind, he'd probably make it to shul in time. Even if he stopped to pick up his friend Aharon, as he usually did, they would be able to walk in just as Shacharis was starting.

The problem was, who wanted to rush like that?

I'll go to a later minyan, he thought, already half asleep again.

Then he remembered — day camp had started. There would be no later *minyan* for him today. It was either this *minyan,* or *daven* alone at home before camp.

An enormous yawn split his face in half. Boy, was he tired! Ever since his bar mitzvah last month, he'd been trying hard to *daven* with a *minyan* every day. But would it be so terrible if he slept in just this once?

Especially since he was so-o-o tired …

Mrs. Harmon picked up her cup of tea and carried it over to the padded rocking chair by the window of her modest apartment.

This was her morning routine. Though her family

was long grown up and gone, and her husband had died a few years earlier, she still woke up at the same time every day and rigidly followed the same pattern. After a simple breakfast, she always spent a few minutes at the front window, watching the world go by.

Mrs. Harmon had a lonely life, but she tried to make the best of it by finding little things that made her happy. One of those things was watching all the different kinds of people who passed by her window in the morning. (She usually took up her post by the window again at the end of the day, when she could enjoy the sight of fathers coming home from work and children playing happily outside before supper.) By now, she could pick out a few familiar faces among the ones that passed her every day.

One of her favorite faces was a fairly new one. About a month before, he'd started coming down her street every morning, a velvet *tefillin* bag under one arm and an eager look in his eye. A new bar mitzvah, she'd guessed with a smile. How excited he looked to be taking his place in a *minyan* along with all the grown-up men!

Though Mrs. Harmon didn't know the boy's name, where he lived, or anything else about him, she'd begun looking forward to seeing him approach her house from the far end of the block at the same time every day. Lately, he usually had a friend with him.

The sight of the boy always cheered her up. Somehow, that young, happy face made her feel that all was right in the world. She might be old and lonely — but when that nice boy came striding down her street on his way to shul, she always had a feeling that it was going to be a good day.

She checked the clock: He was due to appear any time now. She settled herself more comfortably in the rocking chair and waited.

But the minutes ticked past with no sign of the boy she'd grown so used to seeing each day. Other people passed by, looking preoccupied or busy or bored. But there was no boy with the *tefillin* bag under his arm and the eager look in his eye.

Mrs. Harmon sat by the window a little longer than usual that morning, waiting and hoping. But the boy never came.

Finally, the elderly woman turned away from the street. She might try lifting her spirits with a second cup of tea … but she knew it just wouldn't be the same.

"Aharon, wake up! It's time for shul!"

Aharon opened a bleary eye and scowled at his sister. "Go 'way …."

"Mommy said to wake you. Yudi will be here any minute. You have to get up!"

At the mention of Yudi's name, Aharon's head

cleared a bit. He always had a hard time getting up in the morning, but since his friend had started picking him up on the way to *Shacharis* this summer, it was easier. He and Yudi had fun walking to shul together, and then home again afterwards.

He looked at the clock. "He's late."

"So why not get ready anyway?" his sister urged. "That way, he won't have to wait for you like he always does."

It was true. Yudi always had to wait for Aharon — but not for long. Aharon might have a hard time waking up in the morning, but once he *was* up, he could get ready faster than anyone she had ever seen. In no time at all, it seemed, he could be washed and dressed and ready to snatch up his *tefillin* bag and leave for shul with Yudi.

"Tell me when he gets here ...," Aharon mumbled, closing his eyes again. He was fast asleep in two seconds flat.

His sister clicked her tongue in annoyance and went to report to her mother that she'd had no luck with Aharon. She and her mother both kept an ear attuned to the front door, ready to open it for Yudi when he arrived. Then there'd be the usual whirlwind, as Aharon tried not to keep his friend waiting for too long.

But Yudi didn't come.

So Aharon, much to his mother's and sister's disappointment (and, secretly, to his own disappointment as well), davened at home that morning.

The *gabbai* at the shul was a fair man. In assigning the various honors during *Shacharis*, such as *aliyah*s for the Torah reading, he tried to include everyone sooner or later.

Naturally, there were some people who got those honors sooner rather than later. The two or three *kohanim* in the morning *minyan*, for instance, took turns standing up for the first *aliyah*. Other men, respected pillars of the community, regularly received *aliyos*, too. This morning, with summer here, the *minyan* was a little sparser than usual. This would be a good opportunity, the *gabbai* thought, to offer honors to people who didn't usually get them.

Like that nice Stein boy, for instance. Yudi Stein had been faithfully coming to their *Shacharis minyan* ever since his bar mitzvah about a month before. This past week or two he'd been bringing a friend along. The *gabbai* had noticed that Yudi davened in a serious and respectful fashion, before carefully rolling up his *tefillin* and going home. Today, he decided, would be Yudi's turn. Today, Yehudah Leib ben Shmuel would be called up to the Torah.

The *gabbai* watched the door as people began streaming through and putting on their *tallis* and *tefillin.* He waited as long as he could — but Yudi Stein never showed up.

He was disappointed. This would have been a perfect opportunity to finally give the boy an *aliyah.* As he turned away to get ready for *Shacharis*, the *gabbai* wondered why Yudi had stayed away from shul this morning.

Shimon was new in town. His family had moved here just two weeks before, and he still felt painfully like an outsider.

Though he was already fourteen, he'd been held back by an illness when he was younger and would be entering the eighth grade in the fall. He was anxious to start off the year on the right foot. One way to do that would be to have a regular learning *seder* with someone this summer.

The problem was, who? Shimon hadn't started school yet so he didn't know anyone. His father would be far too busy with his new job to learn regularly with him, except very late at night. Shimon didn't want his mother to hire a tutor. He wanted to learn with someone about his own age, so that maybe they could be friends, too. But how to meet such a person?

For a while, Shimon had despaired of finding the answer.

Then, during *Shacharis* one day, he'd noticed a boy

davening on the other side of the shul. The boy was slim and not very tall, so Shimon assumed that he was much younger than himself. But he wore *tefillin*, which meant he was at least thirteen. Shimon watched him surreptitiously as he davened, and he liked what he saw.

The boy looked nice. And he looked like he took his Yiddishkeit seriously. What more could Shimon ask for in a learning partner?

A week passed, while Shimon tried to work up the courage to approach the boy. He assumed the kid had some sort of schedule to follow during the day, but maybe they could meet back here at shul at the end of the afternoon and learn for an hour or two. He practiced at home in front of the mirror, so the question wouldn't sound too awkward.

"I'm looking for a *chavrusa* this summer. Interested?"

Or maybe, "If you're not too busy, maybe we can get together for a learning *seder* every day?"

Or perhaps just a simple, "Wanna learn?"

This morning, Shimon had woken up and realized that he was letting too much time go by. It was time to act on his decision. If the boy said "no," he'd be no worse off than he'd been before. And if he said "yes," then Shimon would suddenly go from not knowing a soul in town to having a regular session with someone who might turn out to be not only a great learning partner, but maybe even a great friend …

Today was the day.

In his eagerness, Shimon almost ran to shul. After waiting so long, it was agony to wait for the boy to appear. Shimon sat in his place, eyes fixed on the shul door. Any minute now, the boy would walk in and start putting on his *tefillin*. The minute *Shacharis* was over, Shimon intended to go over to him and strike up the conversation he'd been dreaming about for so long.

But — to Shimon's intense disappointment — the nice boy never showed up in shul.

Sometimes we do things that leave holes. The holes may be in our own lives or in the lives of other people — even people we don't know! By the end of the day, we can create enough holes to make life look like a slice of Swiss cheese. How sad ...

But it doesn't have to be that way.

Here's what really happened.

On a sunny Monday in July, Yudi Stein overslept.

He cracked open an eye and checked the clock. It was already so late. Why not just turn over in bed and catch a little more shut-eye? He could always *daven* at home today ....

But Yudi was a new bar mitzvah. He was proud of his record of davening with a *minyan* each and every morning. For a whole month, he'd not only stuck to his resolution, but he'd even managed to drag a friend along.

But Yudi had slept through his alarm. If he wanted to make it to shul on time this morning, he'd have to race like the wind ....

Would it be so terrible if he slept in just this once?

He hesitated another second. Then, almost before his eyes were properly open, he was on his feet. On your mark, get set ... go!

Yudi had overslept — but did he let that stop him from doing what he knew was right? Nope. Because who wants a life that looks like a slice of Swiss cheese?

And so, his friend Aharon made it to shul, too.

The *gabbai* gave Yudi an *aliyah*.

Shimon, the new boy, got a brand-new learning partner.

And old Mrs. Harmon had a very good day.

A SECOND CHANCE

I tiptoed to the end of the hall and peeked around the corner.

The short distance to the water fountain was clear. No one was around. With a spurt of speed, I dashed over to the fountain, made a *brachah*, bent over, and drank. Then I sprinted back to the main corridor, at the far end of which I saw a large number of girls milling around. I couldn't tell if *she* was among them or not. But at least I'd managed to get a drink without running into her ...

I'd been looking forward to this eighth-grade Shabbaton for weeks. Eighth-graders from every school in our town — all three of them — were joining together for a weekend of "learning, growing, and fun," as the flyer had put it. It was only Friday afternoon, but I already knew what *my* weekend was going to be like.

Learning and growing — sure.

But fun? With *her* here?

Not on your life.

Trying to look casual, I sauntered back to my classmates. They were about to head for our assigned rooms to start getting ready for Shabbos. I joined them, glad to get away from the girls from the other schools for a while.

Not that I had anything against the other schools — or the students who attended them.

Except for one.

Rina Hartman and I had been in the same class from first through sixth grade. And, for most of that time, we'd been the best of friends.

And I mean *best* friends. As in, "Anywhere you go, I will follow ...."

At least, that's what I thought it meant. Until the fateful Sunday when my whole world came crashing down ...

"Want to go shopping this morning, Mimi?"

I had not been fully awake yet, but these words had the same effect as cold water on my face. I sat up eagerly. "Sure, Ma! I really need something new for *yom tov*."

My mother smiled. "That's what I thought. Be ready at about ten-thirty, okay? I'll leave the baby at home with Daddy and take you and Michali to the mall."

After she left my room, I checked the clock. Only nine-fifteen. I'd have no problem getting ready on time. All I had to do was get dressed, *daven*, have some breakfast ... and one other thing.

I dressed and davened Shacharis, but found that I couldn't wait till after breakfast to get to the fourth thing on my list. Hurrying over to the phone, I dialed the number that I knew nearly as well as my own.

"Hello?"

"Hi, Mrs. Hartman! Is Rina up yet?"

"I'll check …."

After a few minutes that felt like hours, a sleepy-voiced Rina got on the line. "Mimi? Is that you?"

"Yes, it's me. Wake up, Rina! We're going shopping!"

I could almost see her blinking her eyes as she tried to absorb this news.

"Wake *up*," I said again, impatiently. "My mother wants to take Michali and me to the mall today. We're leaving at about ten-thirty. I'm going to look for something new for *yom tov*. And I want you to come along, okay?"

What I expected was the usual "Sure." What I got instead was like some more frigid water on my face.

"I don't think so," my friend said slowly.

"What?" I screeched. "Why not?"

"I have a little cold, and we have that test coming up. I thought I'd stay home and take it easy and do some studying …."

"That's ridiculous!" I burst out.

She sounded taken aback. "Why is it ridiculous?"

"Well, maybe it's not … But I *need* you, Rina! How am I going to choose the right outfit without you there to help me?"

"You'll be fine, Mimi. You'll have your mother and your sister with you."

"Oh, Michali's too young to know what people are wearing. Especially in *New York*." I was nervous enough about spending the upcoming holiday with my New York cousins. They and their friends were always dressed to the nines. This *yom tov*, I wanted to look my very, *very* best!

"I'm sorry, Mimi. I just don't think it's a good idea. I always get a headache when I go shopping, and I really want to lay low this Sunday. And there's that test …"

"The test's not till Tuesday. You'll have all of tomorrow night to study!"

"You know I never do well when I cram all my studying into one night. I really want to start today."

Suddenly, the truth sank in: Rina really didn't intend to come with me.

I'd been so sure that she'd come through. I'd been

certain that my wheedling and coaxing would do the trick.

Only it wasn't working. Not this time.

First I was disappointed. And then I got mad.

"Is that any way to treat a friend?" I asked coldly. "Thinking only of yourself?"

Rina tried to explain. "I told you, you'll be fine without me. You don't really *need* me there, Mimi. You just *want* me there."

"And my wants are no concern of yours?"

"Of course they are! I just can't make it today, that's all." As if to prove her point, she sneezed.

I was not impressed. "If you don't come with me today, Rina," I said with awful solemnity, "I'll know that you don't really consider yourself my best friend. And I won't consider *you* mine!"

"Now, that's *really* ridiculous!" Rina protested.

"Well?" I snapped. "What's it going to be?"

Now she was getting angry, too. "It's not only ridiculous — it's mean. *You're* the one who's thinking only about herself!"

I gripped the phone very tightly. "Is that a 'no'?"

"Yes!"

"Yes — or no?"

"NO!"

"FINE!" I shouted into the phone. "This is — GOOD-BYE!"

And I meant it.

That was last year, in seventh grade. Rina and I did not exchange a single word after that phone call — which was awkward, considering that our class was not all that big. But we managed.

I don't know who was angrier, she or I.

I felt betrayed. I felt that Rina had willfully misunderstood the meaning of friendship for her own selfish reasons.

And Rina? She probably felt that I'd been demanding and unreasonable. But I didn't ask for explanations. After that awful Sunday, I simply crossed her out of my life, so to speak. From being my closest and best friend, she went down to the bottom of the list of people important to me.

As far as I was concerned, Rina Hartman did not exist.

She switched schools in eighth grade, probably because the new school put her in a better position for the high school she wanted to attend. Or maybe it was just to get away from me. We didn't see each other all summer, and I didn't lay eyes on her for the first three months of the new school year.

And now, here we were, stuck at the same Shabbaton together.

Of course, we weren't the only two people here. The place was swarming with eighth-graders. But as far as I was concerned, we might as well have been stranded alone on a desert island. Everywhere I went, there she seemed to be.

I was going to have my work cut out for me this Shabbos, doing my best to avoid Rina Hartman.

Shabbos was just as uncomfortable as I'd expected it to be.

Only by the narrowest good fortune did I escape being put on a team with Rina at one of the question-and-answer games we played. I had to rush into the dining room extra fast to make sure I got a seat as far away from Rina as possible. I spent a lot of time taking quick peeks at her across the room, to check if *she* was looking at *me*. As you might guess, I didn't get very much out of the well-planned activities, and all that delicious Shabbos food seemed to stick in my throat.

At long last, it was time for Havdalah.

As we stood in the darkened dining room, listening to the age-old words, I felt a wave of emotion wash over me. I recognized the feeling.

It was loneliness.

I felt terribly lonely, which was strange, considering that I was standing shoulder-to-shoulder with dozens of other girls my age.

But then, loneliness was nothing new to me. In that dark room, with only the flickering Havdalah candle to provide a spark of light, I admitted the sad truth to myself: I'd been feeling lonely for a long time. In fact, I'd been feeling that way for exactly ten months now.

Loneliness had settled in to be my new best friend at the precise moment when I'd said good-bye to Rina.

Afterwards, we were told to go back to our rooms, change out of our Shabbos clothes, and get ready for a special Motzei Shabbos activity. I glanced around at the roomful of happy, chattering eighth-graders, looking for the one who I wanted to avoid at all cost.

I didn't see her — but I wasn't about to take any chances. Instead of heading for the front door like everybody else, I decided to take a detour through the kitchen and go out the back way.

All went well at first. I made it past the huge, stainless steel refrigerators large enough to walk into, and the counters with the remains of our *shalosh seudos* meal on it. I was just slipping past the big sinks, when a voice boomed in my ear, "How many times do I have to ask you girls to stay out of my kitchen?"

As I turned guiltily to face the cook — who towered over me wearing a white apron and a very annoyed face — she added sarcastically, "Or maybe you two came in here to wash the dishes. Eh?"

"N-no thanks," I gasped. I looked longingly past her to the door.

It was only then that I heard what she'd just said. *You two.*

"M-me, neither," said another voice nearby.

I whirled around. The voice had been familiar. Much *too* familiar ...

"Out, out! I've got work to do!" The cook made a shooing motion with her hands, as if we were a couple of pesky cats instead of two very mortified eighth-graders. We zoomed out of there at lightning speed.

The back door took us to a dark, empty stretch of ground. We could hear the merry chatter of our friends in the distance. Above our heads, a few stars peeked out through the clouds. Where we stood there was lots of silence and hardly any light.

After all my efforts to stay out of Rina's way, here we were. How embarrassing!

I was about to mumble something, anything, and escape from there as fast as I could, when a sudden question struck me. I knew why *I'd* been trying to escape through the kitchen. But — why had Rina?

"You were trying to avoid me, too!" The words spilled out of my mouth before I realized I was saying them out loud.

Rina looked guilty. Then, sheepishly, she nodded. "I was afraid it would be ... awkward."

"Which it certainly is," I said with a twisted smile.

She nodded. I saw a ghost of the same half-smile on her face.

"Well!" I managed to choke out. "It's ... been a while. How's everything?"

"Fine, *baruch Hashem*," she said automatically. "And you?"

"The same."

Silence.

"Well …," I said again. "Guess we'd better go get ready."

"I guess so." She hesitated, and then started moving away. She probably figured I'd wait for her to get far enough ahead so that we wouldn't have to walk together. Which was exactly what I intended to do.

Then something very strange happened. The same wave of emotion that I'd felt at Havdalah came over me again — only this time, it felt a hundred times more intense. Before, I'd been feeling the absence of something I needed. Something precious.

Now, I was standing here and watching it walk away ….

Life doesn't always give us a second chance, but I was facing one now.

I had a choice. I could do nothing and maintain the situation I'd created the first time around, in that awful phone call. Or …

"*Wait!*" I called. And if there was a slightly frantic note in my voice, I wouldn't have been at all surprised.

She turned around, still close enough to hear me. "What?"

"Um … mind if we walk together?"

Rina looked surprised. "Why?"

I shrugged. "Why not?"

Suddenly, the absurdity of the conversation struck both of us at the same time. We'd always shared the same sense of humor, and it got the better of us now. We laughed until we cried ... and cried until we laughed. I got a stitch in my side and doubled over, clutching my middle. Feeling strangely breathless, I gasped for air.

"Are you okay?" Rina asked anxiously.

Slowly, I straightened up. It still hurt, but the pain was bearable. The breathless feeling was still there, though.

I drew some air into my lungs, both for breathing purposes and for courage, and looked my old friend in the eye. "I am now," I said.

And then Rina and I walked on together, to see what the rest of that extraordinary weekend might bring.

THE
FAVOR

The Brown family was enjoying a quiet Sunday afternoon, when the peace was suddenly shattered by the sound of raised voices.

In the living room, Mr. and Mrs. Brown exchanged a startled glance. Malky, doing homework in her room, lifted her head and listened. Leah and Chani, playing with their dollhouse, paused in their game to wonder what was going on.

Only Dassi wasn't home. But had she been, she doubtless would've also wondered why her brother Shlomo and his best friend Gedalia were yelling at each other like that.

It had all started nearly a week before — on Monday morning, to be exact. Gedalia had an unpleasant shock when his *rebbi* announced, "Next Monday, we will be having a Gemara test ...."

His *rebbi* went on to explain which material the class needed to study, but Gedalia was hardly listening. He was in panic mode.

The reason he was panicking was because Gemara was not his strong point. He *wanted* to do well on the test — but he wasn't sure he had what it took. It wasn't long before he reached the logical conclusion: He needed help.

After *shiur*, he ambled over to his best friend, Shlomo. Gedalia was built like a scarecrow, tall and skinny, with a somewhat pointy nose and a friendly grin. His friend was shorter, sturdier ... and a lot smarter. In fact, Shlomo was the class brain. Especially in Gemara.

"Hey, Gedalia," Shlomo greeted him, gathering up his books and stuffing them into his knapsack. "I'm getting my braces this week. After that, I won't be able to eat sticky stuff like taffy and gum for a long time. Want to stop off at the candy store on the way home?"

"Fine with me." Gedalia fell into step beside his friend. "Uh ... can I ask you a favor?"

"Sure." Shlomo eyed him curiously.

"You know that big Gemara test next Monday? Do you think we could study together?"

Before Shlomo could answer, Gedalia rushed in again, talking quickly. "You probably already know the stuff cold. I know you don't really need to study with me, or with anyone. But … I sure could use the help." He paused, partly for breath, and partly to gauge his friend's reaction.

Shlomo shrugged. "Sure, why not? We can study together. It'll be fun."

"Great!" Gedalia felt as if a huge weight had rolled off his shoulders. Apologetically, he added, "My father's going to be out of town for most of the week, or I'd ask him."

"No problem," Shlomo said. They'd reached the candy store, and his mind was filled with the all-important question of how to best spend the last couple of dollars in his pocket.

As for Gedalia, he didn't need candy. Now that Shlomo had promised to study with him, life was already sweet enough.

By Tuesday morning Shlomo had pretty much forgotten about both the Gemara test and his friend's request. Life was full of so many interesting things to think about. Rebbi started going over the test material, but Shlomo had no intention of starting his own studying yet. There was plenty of time.

Gedalia hadn't really expected Shlomo to start studying that day. Still, there was a wistful moment or two when he wished his friend could see what it felt like to be him. To be scared stiff of a test, and to feel helpless about getting on top of the material without some help …

But Shlomo *didn't* know what that felt like — because he was Shlomo. The class genius wouldn't be bothered by things like that. And that was the reason Gedalia had asked for his help in the first place, right?

Wednesday. It was a rainy day, so recess was indoors. Gedalia thought it was a perfect opportunity to pick up a Gemara and get started on studying with Shlomo. After all, the test was only five days away.

Then someone came over and started asking Shlomo riddles. Shlomo was clearly enjoying the mental puzzle of solving them. Shlomo didn't need five days to study. How could Gedalia ask him to give up his recess just because he, Gedalia, was nervous?

So he said nothing. The bell rang and class went on. Maybe Shlomo would suggest that they meet after school to start studying, Gedalia thought hopefully.

But the last bell came and went, and then Shlomo's mother came to take him to the orthodontist to be fitted for his new braces.

"Good luck," Gedalia called as his friend got in the car.

"Thanks." Shlomo looked a little nervous. He wasn't at all sure he was going to like walking around in braces for the next two years.

The car door slammed. Gedalia started walking home alone. Not a word had been said about the Gemara test.

Thursday morning, Gedalia woke up and thought, *Today's the day.* Surely today Shlomo would suggest that they get together and finally crack open a Gemara.

But Shlomo was in a grumpy mood all day because his new braces were uncomfortable. He spoke as little as possible to keep them hidden, and when spoken to, he would answer in a growl. Even Gedalia thought it prudent to keep his distance. Shlomo went straight home after school, clearly not in the mood for anything or anybody.

That night, Gedalia opened his Gemara at home and tried to make some headway on his own. It was uphill work. At the end of an hour, he didn't feel like he'd come very far at all.

There were just three more studying days left. He was starting to feel desperate.

On Friday, Gedalia finally mustered the courage to broach the subject.

"The test's on Monday," he said diffidently, as if this was a big surprise instead of the one thing he'd been thinking about almost non-stop all week. "Wanna study on Shabbos?"

"Hmm?" The braces were feeling a little better now, and Shlomo had been dreaming about all the sweet, sticky goodies he was going to eat as soon as they came off.

"Shabbos. Gemara. Study," Gedalia said patiently.

"Oh, you want to study on Shabbos? Fine."

Gedalia heaved a sigh of relief. If they spent both Shabbos and Sunday afternoons with their *gemara*s, he still had a chance of doing pretty well on the test. He was counting the minutes.

Shlomo had every intention of studying with Gedalia on Shabbos afternoon. How was he supposed to know that two kids from the neighborhood would decide to drop in for a visit right after the Shabbos *seudah*?

The three boys were deeply involved in a board game when they heard a knock at the front door. Shlomo looked up. "I'll get it. It's probably Gedalia."

It *was* Gedalia. His friend greeted him with a big smile and an eager, "Ready to start learning?"

"Uh … we've got a little problem."

Peering over Shlomo's shoulder, Gedalia saw what the problem was. His face darkened. "Why'd you invite them over?" he hissed.

"I didn't. They just decided to come by. What was I supposed to do — send them away?"

"But you agreed to study with *me* today!" Gedalia was agitated.

"I'm sure they'll be leaving soon," Shlomo whispered back.

But the two other boys didn't leave soon. In fact, they stayed right up to *shalosh seudos* and then happily accepted Mrs. Brown's invitation to stay for the meal.

All afternoon, Gedalia stewed. Here it was, just two days before the big test, and he'd hardly studied at all yet! What a waste of a good Shabbos afternoon! How could Shlomo *do* this to him?

Still, there was always tonight.

The minute Havdalah was over, the other boys went to the window to wait for their parents' cars. Gedalia pulled Shlomo aside. "What about our studying?"

Shlomo was about to say something when his mother poked her head through the kitchen door. "Shlomo, don't forget to change your shirt before we leave. You got some cholent on the sleeve today, remember?"

"Sure, Ma."

Mrs. Brown withdrew her head. Gedalia stared at Shlomo. "Leave? Where are you going?"

"My grandparents' anniversary party. I forgot all about it." Shlomo looked chagrined.

Gedalia counted to ten, trying to calm himself. His nerves felt as though someone had pulled them out and twisted them into a big ball. Tomorrow was the *last day before the test*!

"What about tomorrow?" he managed to ask.

"*Bli neder*, we'll get together right after school and study. In fact, why don't you come over straight from school and have lunch here? That'll give us a head start."

"Okay." Gedalia's heart was still pounding. "It's a plan."

But plans sometimes have a way of going awry. At recess the next morning Shlomo came over to Gedalia and said, "Sorry about this, but my mom wants to take me shopping for pants right after school. She says it's the only time she can do it." Seeing the look on his friend's face, he added quickly, "It'll only be an hour or so. I'll call you the minute I get back."

All the way home, Gedalia was kicking himself. He should have known better than to count on Shlomo! The class genius had no idea how it felt to be in a total panic over a test. The Gemara came so easily to him that he had no sense of urgency about it at all. In fact, he probably knew the material cold already. He probably didn't even *need* to study!

True to his word, Shlomo — now the proud owner of two new pairs of pants — called Gedalia the moment he got home. Gedalia was at his door ten minutes after that. The two boys went up to Shlomo's room with their *gemaras*.

But they weren't studying. They were fighting.

Throughout the house, the Browns listened … and wondered.

"Should I go up there?" Mr. Brown said to his wife. "They sound like they could use some help."

"Wait a bit," she advised. "Maybe they'll resolve it on their own."

Sure enough, the voices stopped.

Soon after, however, they started up again ….

In Shlomo's room, he and Gedalia glared at each other.

"How was *I* supposed to know you were feeling so nervous about the test?" Shlomo demanded.

"If you had an ounce of imagination, you'd have known," Gedalia insisted furiously. "Why do you think I asked you to study with me the day the test was announced — a whole week before? I'm not just nervous. I'm terrified!"

"You should have said something!"

"You should have known!"

They glared at each other some more. Shlomo

was breathing hard. Gedalia's throat was hoarse from shouting. He'd never exploded at his friend like this before. In fact, he'd hardly ever been this mad at *anyone* before! He'd been counting on Shlomo — and Shlomo had let him down.

There was a tap on the door. Mr. Brown stuck his head into the room. "Can I help with anything, boys?"

Only a year ago, they probably would have just shaken their heads. Now they were old enough to know that sometimes people do need help resolving things. And this seemed to be one of those times.

So Mr. Brown came in, prepared to listen. Gedalia told his side of the story first, and then Shlomo told his.

"Let me see if I've got this straight," Shlomo's father said when they were done. "Gedalia, you were hoping that Shlomo would have realized how desperate you were to study and would have offered to do it days ago. You're feeling let down and disappointed."

"*And* terrified of failing the test," Gedalia added darkly.

Mr. Brown nodded. He turned to his son. "And you claim that you had no idea Gedalia was feeling this way. You aren't nervous about the test. You know that one afternoon of studying will do the trick."

"For *him*, maybe," Gedalia muttered.

Mr. Brown nodded again. He eyed his son, and waited.

Shlomo looked at his father's expectant face, and

then at his friend's troubled one. He swallowed hard.

"I'm sorry," he told Gedalia. "I guess I should have realized."

Gedalia looked gratified, and then ashamed. "I'm sorry, too."

Shlomo was surprised. "You? Why?"

"Because I expected you to know how I felt without my having to tell you. I wanted you to read my mind." He grinned sheepishly. "Not so realistic, huh?"

Mrs. Brown looked up at her husband. "Is everything okay up there?"

"A-okay. Fight resolved, and important lessons learned. They're sitting with their *gemara*s now, working hard."

Up in his room, Shlomo was trying to make up for the pain he'd caused his friend by giving this study session everything he had. And it didn't take a mind reader to know that Gedalia, for the first time all week, had moved out of panic mode.

His face wore an intent expression, not a frightened one. He wasn't thinking about whether or not he would pass the Gemara test. He was just learning Gemara.

Downstairs, Mr. and Mrs. Brown relished the silence.

In their rooms, Malky, Leah, and Chani went back

to what they were doing, also enjoying the peace that had been restored to their home.

All was quiet now — except for the lively sound of two young voices in the room down the hall. Voices that had been raised in anger and recrimination just a short time before — now joined in friendship and Torah.

A LETTER
FROM BAILY

"This is so-o-o annoying!" Raizy fumed.

Her mother looked up from her crocheting. "What is?"

"I've been trying and trying to call Cousin Leah in Israel, but the circuits keep being busy!"

Raizy looked frustrated. Her mother looked amused.

"What's so funny?" Raizy asked.

"I can remember a time when a long-distance call to Israel was so expensive, people only called their families once or twice a year."

"Really?" Raizy's eyes grew round.

"Really. And there was no such thing as email. People had to sit down and write an old-fashioned letter, which took days to reach its destination."

"Well, I'm glad I live *now* and not *then*," Raizy declared. "I don't have the patience to wait that long!"

"Neither did I ...," Ma murmured. There was a far-off gleam in her eye. She looked at her daughter. "Want to hear a story? It happened to me — way back in 'ancient times,' when people wrote letters to each other and then had to wait ... and wait ... and sometimes wait some more for an answer."

"Sure!" Raizy loved a good story. Abandoning the phone and its annoyingly busy circuits, she plopped herself down on the couch beside her mother.

"I was thirteen years old when the story took place," Ma began. "Or rather, thirteen minus one week ..."

I opened the door and ushered my friends into my house. After a brief stop in the kitchen for snacks, we went to my room, which felt rather crowded with all five of us in there at the same time.

"Oh, look!" I squealed happily. "A letter from Baily!"

"Who's Baily?" my friend Nechama asked.

"Don't you remember? She's my friend from camp. We've been writing each other back and forth for the past few months, ever since the summer."

"Where does she live?"

"In Milwaukee. Our parents didn't like the idea of long-distance phone calls — you should see our phone bill, even without them! — so we decided to be pen pals instead." I smiled and picked up the envelope that my mother had left on my desk. "It's fun."

"What does she say?" Yael asked curiously.

I scanned the letter's opening paragraphs. "Well, she sends her best regards to all of you. I told her all about you guys in my letters. She says she feels like she knows you already."

I folded the page and put it back in its envelope. I'd finish reading it later. Right now we had something important to discuss.

"About my birthday," I began.

My friends sat up, electrified. There's nothing more fun than planning a birthday party. Except that I wasn't about to have a real party. I'd had a big family bash for my bas mitzvah the year before; this year I wanted to do something different to celebrate.

"Here's the story," I said. "My parents are willing to take all of us somewhere next Sunday, the day before my actual birthday. All we have to do is decide where!"

We put on our thinking caps. It was June, a good season for an outdoor activity. Then Ahuva reminded us about an amusement park about ninety minutes away. "I hear they've got a brand-new roller coaster!" she said. "It's supposed to be really scary."

"Sounds like fun," Yael said, eyes sparkling. Yael loved roller coasters.

But some of my other friends liked different things

more. We finally narrowed our decision down to two choices: roller-skating at an indoor rink followed by pizza and ice cream, or the amusement park with its new roller coaster. Back and forth we went, arguing and re-arguing, hashing over the merits of each choice and then the reasons why the other choice might be better.

Finally, in frustration, Chani exclaimed, "I wish someone would just make the decision for us!"

That gave me an idea. I turned to my friends with a mischievous grin. "Are you *all* willing to let someone else decide for us?"

"Someone?" Nechama asked. "Like who?"

"Like Baily! I could write her a letter right now, asking her to decide between these two options. Whatever she says we'll do. Agreed?"

There was something exciting about the idea of throwing the question to my friend in far-away Milwaukee and waiting to hear what she'd say. My friends all agreed to the plan.

"Okay," I said. "I'll write her right now. But remember, whatever Baily says, goes. Right?"

"Right!" the girls chorused.

I sat down to compose the letter to my camp friend.

Dear Baily,

I know I owe you a real letter, and bli neder I'll write you a long one next week, after my birth-

day. Right now we've got a problem — and we've decided that you're the one who's going to solve it for us!

I went on to describe the two options we were considering for my birthday outing: the amusement park, or roller-skating and pizza.

It's up to you, Baily, I continued. *Today's Sunday. I'll mail this letter tomorrow morning. It should reach you by Wednesday. If you write right back with your decision, we'll get the answer by Friday — or Shabbos, at the latest. That way we'll know exactly what we'll be doing on Sunday!*

Remember: Write back with your decision <u>as soon as you get this</u>. We'll do whatever YOU decide!

I looked up. "Finished. I'll get a stamp and envelope on my way downstairs."

My friends nodded their approval. The decision was out of our hands.

Then we remembered the snacks lying untouched on my desk. We fell on them as if we hadn't seen food in a month.

I'd forgotten how hard waiting can be.

When I dropped my letter in the mailbox on Monday morning, I knew it would be at least four days before I received an answer. Four endless days ...

I toyed with the idea of asking my parents if I could make a quick long-distance call to Baily, to speed things up. But they'd already told me that they didn't want me making those kinds of calls, and I didn't want to bother them about it now — especially when they were already being so nice about taking all of us out for my birthday.

Besides, though the wait was hard, it also added spice to the week. I woke up each morning mentally crossing one day off the waiting time. In school, it was all my friends and I could talk about.

What would Baily decide?

"Did you get an answer yet?" my friends started asking me on Wednesday.

"No," I replied patiently. "Baily probably just got my letter today. Patience ..."

But my friends *weren't* patient. To tell the truth, neither was I. And my parents weren't happy with the wait, either.

"Your father and I would like to be able to start making plans for Sunday," my mother told me on Thursday night. "Which will it be — the amusement park, or the skating rink and pizza?"

I bit my lip — and told her about our plan.

My mother stared at me. "You're going to let your friend from camp decide for you?"

I nodded.

"Will her answer get here in time?"

"I told her to write back the minute she got my letter. I should have her answer by tomorrow." In a smaller voice I added, "Or Shabbos, at the latest."

"Which doesn't leave us much time to get ready," my mother said disapprovingly.

I held my breath.

"Okay. We'll wait. Or ..." She eyed me as a new thought struck her. "Do you want to put off your birthday outing till next week?"

"No way!" I said quickly. "Baily will write back right away. I know she will."

Silently, I changed that to: *I hope she will ...*

No letter came on Friday.

My friends were disappointed — but not as disappointed as I was. I could see that my parents were starting to feel impatient, too.

"Maybe we should just decide ourselves?" Ahuva asked. The other girls looked as if they weren't sure what they thought about this.

"It's not a problem," I said confidently. "Baily's a very reliable girl. There was probably a problem with the mail delivery or something. I'm absolutely certain the answer will come tomorrow. On Motzei Shabbos, right after Havdalah, I'll open the letter — and we'll know what we're doing for my birthday!"

It was *my* birthday, so my friends had no choice but to acquiesce.

That was the longest Shabbos I ever lived through.

The minute Havdalah was over, I dashed out to the mailbox. Imagine my chagrin when there was no envelope with Baily's handwriting on the front!

"You're the birthday girl, so you decide. Which one is it going to be?" my father asked.

I called my friends. After about a million calls, we still couldn't decide which we wanted to do more. So my parents decided for me.

"Skating and pizza," my mother said. "It's closer, and it's easier."

"Not to mention less expensive," my father added.

I nodded my head, feeling strangely let down. I wouldn't have minded if Baily had written with the same decision. But having our little game fall through was disappointing.

Forcing a smile into my voice, I called my friends with the news.

My birthday outing was fun. But in the back of my mind — in the back of all of our minds, maybe — was a tiny part that kept wondering if we wouldn't have had an even better time at the amusement park.

And I fell asleep that night wondering something else: Why hadn't Baily come through for me?

I was still wondering that as I walked into our classroom the next morning. Yael waved at me urgently from across the room. Listlessly, I waved back. Monday is definitely not my favorite day of the week. Five whole days of school ahead of me, and no more birthday celebration to look forward to. Life felt a little flat.

Yael rushed over to my desk as I was taking out my notebooks. She was very pale. "Look at this." She held out an article torn from the newspaper.

"What ...?" I started to ask.

"Just read it." There was something grim and almost frightening in Yael's face. After a last, curious glance at her, I lowered my eyes to the article.

The first thing I saw was the photo that accompanied the article. It showed two pictures, side by side. The first was of a gleaming new roller coaster soaring proudly up into the sky.

The second showed the same ride with a big chunk of it broken and mangled.

The headline beneath the twin photos read: "Tragedy at the Amusement Park."

I read the article quickly, my heart thumping. It seemed the new roller coaster we'd been so eager to ride had not been put together properly. Yesterday — Sunday, the day of my birthday outing — a portion had broken in mid-ride, throwing several people to the ground below. Two of them had been gravely injured.

Yael met my eyes. She looked stricken. I'm sure I looked the same way.

Without a word I walked away to find our other friends. I showed them the article. The five of us stood in a hushed circle, thinking thoughts that suddenly felt too big for our heads.

"I was a little disappointed yesterday," Chani whispered. "The whole time we were skating, I kept thinking about how much fun that roller coaster would have been."

"Me, too," Nechama said. She was as pale as Yael had been a moment earlier.

"Can I take this home?" I asked Yael, holding up the article with the before-and-after pictures. "I want to show my parents."

Yael nodded solemnly and shuddered. "You can keep it."

As I walked into the house after school that day, my mother greeted me: "Your friend's letter came today."

Wordlessly, I showed her the article.

Then I went upstairs, to read the letter that had come too late.

Sorry I didn't write sooner! Baily wrote in her usual, breathless style. *I meant to sit down and answer your letter the second I got it — but you'll never believe what happened! As I was walking upstairs to my room, I somehow slipped and fell! And my wrist got sprained!!!*

I was in so much pain that I forgot all about writing. My mother took me to the emergency room, where they bandaged it up and put my arm in a sling. It was killing me all night!!!

I'm really sorry, but all the excitement (and the PAIN!) made me forget about the letter until Friday afternoon. This probably won't reach you before your birthday outing, but I'm writing my decision here anyway, just in case ...

I say you should go to the amusement park! That new roller coaster sounds amazing!

Let me know what happens, okay?

Love,

Baily

Ma gazed at Raizy. Raizy gazed back at her mother, her eyes rounder than ever.

"Because Baily hurt her wrist ...," she began.

"We didn't go on that roller coaster," Ma finished for her.

"Imagine if Baily's letter hadn't come too late!

You were planning to do whatever she said!"

Ma looked at her daughter. "We thought it was going to be Baily who chose what happened that Sunday," she said quietly. "But she didn't get to choose at all."

"Right. Your parents did."

"Not really." Ma smiled. At Raizy's puzzled look, she added, "Hashem did."

Raizy nodded thoughtfully. Then she made a face. "Just like He's choosing to make the circuits to Israel busy today?"

"Yes."

"But why? What do I need this aggravation for?"

Ma picked up her crocheting again. "I imagine," she said, "that Baily asked the very same question when she fell down and sprained her wrist ... Wouldn't you agree?"

SMALL PACKAGES

This is not really my story. It's my brother's.
Until a few weeks ago, I wouldn't have even known that my younger brother *had* a story to tell. Hilly is not the kind of kid you find standing in the spotlight. In fact, he's not the kind of kid you notice much at all — at least, not at first. He's on the small side and tends to get overlooked a lot. It's only when you get to know him that you realize just how much great stuff can be packed into one small frame ….

Hilly's height used to bother him, I know. The only time I ever teased him by calling him "Shorty," I was taken aback to see his face turn completely white, though whether it was from hurt or anger I'll never know. He didn't cry, but his eyes had such a stricken look that, in a rush of remorse, I blurted, "Sorry, Hilly. I won't ever say that again." And I didn't.

When he was about seven or eight and the other kids started teasing him about his height — or lack of it — I once heard Hilly complain to our *zeidy*. "It's not fair! All the other kids are taller than I am. Why'd Hashem make me so short?"

Zeidy is kind of on the short side himself. He chuckled, gave Hilly a fond smile, and said, "Well, you know what they say, Hilly: 'Good things come in small packages'!"

I could tell that my brother wasn't very satisfied with that answer. But Zeidy distracted him with a funny joke, and then Bubby came in with some freshly baked cookies, and the moment passed ... though not the problem.

The day Hilly stopped worrying about his height was the day he kicked a ball across an entire soccer field with such strength that it whizzed into the goal like a guided missile. I happened to be in the park at the time, and I saw it with my own eyes. His friends stared for a split second, and then burst into the loudest cheers you ever heard.

Hilly looked startled, as if he hadn't known he had it in him. Then the world's biggest smile crept over his face. Small he might be, but he was a powerhouse —

and he had terrific aim. In the world of schoolboys, that counts for a lot!

Once he discovered that he had a talent for sports, Hilly became a regular at the after-school games that the other boys were always playing on the long spring nights. He was still on the quiet side and didn't like drawing attention to himself. But by the time he hit seventh grade, he'd found his niche. He was an okay student and a good athlete, and he had a nice circle of friends. Hilly was a contented kid.

And then his rebbi announced a new twist on their annual Lag B'Omer outing ... and Hilly's contentment flew out the window.

I didn't know a thing about it at first. Being in the ninth grade, I get home from school later than my brother, so I didn't get to see his face as he walked through the door. My mother did, though, and she described it to me afterwards. Hilly, she said, looked as if he'd just lost his best friend.

It wasn't until later that I discovered it was even worse than that.

Hilly was quiet during dinner, but that wasn't so unusual. My sisters kept up a steady flow of chatter, and when *they* weren't talking I was telling my father all about the Gemara test we'd had that day. Hilly's silence went pretty much unnoticed, though Ma did throw an anxious look at him now and then.

After dinner, Hilly disappeared into his room, presumably to do his homework. I drifted back up to my own, where I wasted most of the evening before finally deciding to crack the books. Vaguely, I heard the phone ring and someone pick up downstairs. When I went down a little later to get a drink, I could hear the occasional murmur as my father spoke with someone. Mostly, though, he just listened ....

I got my drink and was halfway up the stairs again when I heard my name.

"Meir," my father said quietly from the door of the den, where he'd been speaking on the phone, "please come in here. I want to talk to you."

I followed him into the den and found my mother already there. Curious, I looked from one to the other, wondering what this was all about.

"I just got a call from Hilly's rebbi at school," Ta said slowly. "It seems there was ... quite a scene in their class today."

"A scene?" I was puzzled. My brother is the last person I'd ever associate with making scenes. "Involving Hilly?"

Dryly, my father said, "*Starring* Hilly!"

I stared at my father. Ta sat down with a sigh. "I'm sharing this with you, Meir, because you're old enough to be able to help him. He's going through a rough time now, through no fault of his own. I want you to be extra sensitive to him, and maybe even spend some of your free time together. I don't think we'll be seeing much of his classmates for a while ...."

"Why not?" I asked in surprise.

"Hilly," Ta said sadly, "has suddenly become the class pariah."

"The class *what*?"

"Pariah," Ta said. "Outcast. An undesirable."

"But *why*?" I couldn't even imagine a scenario that would cast my harmless younger brother in that role.

"I'll tell you," my father said. "It happened like this ...."

The three boys wore identical, glowering faces as they watched Nochum Ringel walk away.

"He's always giving us mussar," Bentzy growled.

"Who does he think he is?" Shloimy asked.

"Yesterday," Moishy said, "he told me I was making my brachos too fast."

"He told me I need to daven with more kavanah," Bentzy said.

"He's always criticizing everything we do," Shloimy complained.

Bentzy narrowed his eyes. "There must be some way we can teach that Nochum a lesson ...."

Nothing occurred to any of the three boys right then. It wasn't until the end of the morning, when their rebbi made his special announcement, that the brainstorm came.

"Boys!" Rabbi Spiegel boomed in his hearty way. "This year, for our Lag B'Omer trip, I thought of a new idea. A friend of mine, Rabbi Newman, teaches the seventh grade at Yeshivas Chachmei Torah. How about if we have a soccer playoff in the park — us against them?"

Deafening cheers told him that his class liked the idea.

"Okay." He smiled. "I'm going to pick a captain for our side. The captain will be in charge of whipping you boys into a team that can give you boys the best chance of winning against Chachmei Torah!" He looked around. "Any nominations?"

Bentzy looked around, too. He noticed Nochum Ringel's empty seat, and remembered that Nochum had left early for a dentist appointment. A gleam came into his eye. What an idea!

Quickly, he raised his hand. "I nominate ... Nochum Ringel!"

There was a stir in the classroom. One or two boys burst out laughing, but Bentzy's pointed glare soon silenced them. They all knew that Nochum was the most un-athletic kid in the class. Tall, spindly, and bespectacled, he could hardly connect with a soccer ball, let alone lead a team to victory.

Bentzy's friends, Shloimy and Moishy, grasped what

he was doing. "I second the motion!" Shloimy cried. And Moishy waved his hand wildly, saying, "He'd make a great captain!"

"Nochum Ringel?" Rebbi repeated doubtfully. He hadn't known that Nochum even knew how to play soccer.

But the three boys were nodding their heads vigorously, and some of their classmates soon followed suit. The rest of the class held their tongues, intimidated by Bentzy's frowns and the trio's united strength.

"Are you sure he's the right person?" Rabbi Spiegel asked. "I mean, we want to play a great game, right? So we need to put forth our best effort."

Winning against Chachmei Torah would be nice — but not as nice as seeing Nochum Ringel make a complete laughingstock of himself. He deserved it! Bentzy, Moishy, and Shloimy were not the only ones who'd had a taste of Nochum's preaching. Nochum had no real friends in the class, which was not really surprising as his favorite activity seemed to be pointing out everyone's faults.

And so, when Rebbi asked for a show of hands to see how much support there was for Bentzy's nomination, nearly everyone raised his hand. The seventh grade wanted to win — but, even more, they wanted to see the despised Nochum get his comeuppance, once and for all ....

"All right, then," Rebbi said. He was surprised at the class's choice for team captain, but the decision did seem to be more or less unanimous. "Nochum it is."

He was about to dismiss the class when there was

a sudden movement in the front row. *The shortest kids in the class occupied that row, and it was the very shortest — my brother Hilly — who slowly rose to his feet now.*

"Rebbi," *he said. The words sounded choked, as if they were fighting their way out of his throat.* "This is a mistake."

"Mistake?" *Rebbi repeated, puzzled.*

"Yes." *Hilly drew a deep breath.* "Nochum Ringel is definitely not captain material. He would hate it. He would do an awful job." *Hilly turned his head briefly to glance at Bentzy and his friends.* "And every single person here knows it!"

A sudden, intense silence fell over the classroom. It was like an invisible curtain — or maybe a wall — dropping down from nowhere.

A wall of iron, dividing my brother Hilly from the rest of his outraged class.

"Rabbi Spiegel asked some questions and found out what was really going on," my father said. "Of course, he was very upset with the boys who had perpetrated the nasty joke — *and* with the rest of the class for going along with it. They'd chosen a time when Nochum wasn't there to create a situation where he would be sure to fall flat on his face. And only Hilly had the courage to stand up and tell it like it is."

"I'm proud of him," Ma said softly. There were tears in her eyes.

Now I understood the meaning of Hilly's silence all evening. Wouldn't *you* be silent, too, if your entire class was furious with you?

But I still didn't get it. "Wasn't there *anyone* who agreed with Hilly? Were they all that mean?"

"I'm sure there were boys who felt the same way Hilly did," Ta said. "But they were afraid to speak up. According to Bentzy and his friends, Hilly betrayed the class. They were all in on this together, and he gave them away. Anyone who dares side with Hilly now will be labeled a traitor, too."

I stood up. "I'm going up to talk to him."

"I doubt he'll want to talk," Ma said. "He needs some time to recover. But I'm sure he'll appreciate your company more than ever, now that his classmates have turned their backs on him."

And they kept their backs turned.

For the next week, no one called Hilly or came over to play with him. No one invited him over or asked if he wanted to study together. It was as if Hilly had become invisible. Non-existent. A pariah … The seventh grade was out to punish my brother, and he was taking it hard.

He tried not to show it, but the strain was making him miserable. When a citywide power outage gave us an early dismissal one afternoon, Hilly walked home at my side in gloomy silence. Impulsively, I said, "Hilly, want to go bike riding?"

He looked surprised. "Right now?"

"Why not? We have some unexpected free time. Let's make the most of it!"

So we got our bikes out of the garage, said good-bye to our mother, and off we went.

Without discussing it, we both knew where we were headed: Greenwood Park. It has the best biking trails. And when you get tired of biking, there's a nice pond with some comfortable benches nearby. About ten minutes of hard riding got us there. We turned right and started down one of the paths.

We'd hardly rounded the first curve of the pond when another small group of bikers came into view. Behind me, I heard Hilly gasp. Twisting my head to look over my shoulder, I called, "What's the problem?"

"Quick, let's go the other way," he hissed.

I looked at the group again. This time, I recognized one or two of the boys. They were seventh-graders — in Hilly's class.

"Let's *go*," Hilly pleaded. He started turning around.

He whizzed past me, back in the direction we'd just come from. I was about to follow suit when I heard someone give a shout. An instant later, the four bikers were coming our way.

Hilly pedaled even faster. The boys gave chase. I

brought up the rear, wondering how all of this was going to end. Were his classmates planning a concerted attack on my helpless brother?

No — he wasn't helpless. He had *me*. Putting on a spurt of speed, I made my determined way after them. I caught up just as the bikers reached Hilly. In a moment, he was surrounded.

One boy got off his bike.

"Hi, Hilly," he said. He didn't sound very threatening.

"H-hi, Yossi," Hilly answered uncertainly.

"We just wanted to say that ..." Yossi's voice trailed away.

Someone else finished for him. "You were pretty brave the other day ...."

"When you told Rebbi what was happening. About Nochum Ringel," another boy clarified.

"We shouldn't have gone along with Bentzy," the fourth said sadly.

"Or treated you the way we did," Yossi added, hanging his head.

There were a few beats of silence as Hilly stared around at them.

"You really mean that, guys?" he asked, as if he couldn't believe his ears.

The fourth boy's head came up with a jerk. "Sure, we mean it!"

"Wanna ride with us?" Yossi asked.

Hilly glanced over at me, a question in his eyes. It was a question I knew the answer to without even trying.

"Sure. Go ahead!" I said with a genial wave. "Have fun!"

The last I saw of Hilly, he was riding down the biking trail in the center of a group of friends — and in a blaze of glory.

That's my brother. He may be short on inches, but his spirit towers higher than many people taller and older than he is. And now his classmates knew it, too.

As I watched him ride away, there was a big smile on my face and plenty of respect in my heart. Everyone has a story, and this one is Hilly's.

I turned my bike around and started pedaling for home. I couldn't wait to tell my parents the good news!

BUBBLES

All across the auditorium, you could have heard a pin drop. The only sound in the big room was Devorah's voice, and the occasional rustle as she turned a page.

She was very nervous at first. Standing up on the stage all alone, facing every single girl in her school — *and* her teachers and principals — was one of the hardest things she'd ever done.

It was easier once she started reading. The words flowed from her mouth in a clear, steady stream. Devorah read that story exactly the way it should be read. And why not? She was the one who'd written it, after all.

She still could hardly believe this was happening.

The story should have been sitting in the bottom drawer of her desk at home, along with all the others that she'd written over the years. The ones at the very bottom of the pile were in the stiff, childish handwriting she'd had in second grade. In the middle of the pile were the loopy scripts and misspelled words of the middle grades. And closer to the top were the stories she'd written last year, in seventh grade, and earlier this year, in eighth. They were pretty good stories, she thought.

But none of them were as good as "Bubbles."

And that wasn't only Devorah's opinion — or she wouldn't be standing here right now, reading her story out loud to the whole school.

"Anyone who'd like to enter the contest should submit her story by the fifteenth of this month," their English teacher had announced at the end of class one day, about two months earlier.

Devorah, who'd been daydreaming as usual, startled awake. "What contest?" she whispered to her friend Naomi.

Naomi rolled her eyes, as if to say, *Why can't you ever pay attention?*

"Tell you later," she whispered back.

Later, at recess, she did tell her. "There's going to

be a statewide writing contest," Naomi said. "Short stories. Interested?"

Devorah's sparkling eyes were all the answer she needed.

The two girls started walking home. They'd been walking home together for the past few months, ever since Naomi had moved into Devorah's neighborhood. They'd also chosen to sit beside each other in class, were study partners for most of their tests, and spent nearly all their Shabbos and Sunday afternoons together.

How Naomi felt about their friendship, Devorah didn't know. For her part, she was thrilled. All her life she'd longed to have a best friend. She still could hardly believe that she really had one now!

Her best friend was talking as they walked, but Devorah didn't really hear her. She was deeply absorbed in the pictures she saw in her own mind. She was creating a story.

"Hey!" The sharpness in Naomi's voice finally roused Devorah from her imaginings. "You weren't listening to a thing I said!"

Devorah couldn't deny it. "Sorry about that. I'm starting to plan my story for the contest," she explained.

"Can you do me a favor and wait till you get home? Honestly! I might as well be walking alone!"

Devorah apologized again and did her best to tune in to Naomi all the rest of the way.

It wasn't easy. Her imagination wanted to carry her away to wondrous places, far, far away from the humdrum city streets.

It wasn't until she was safely in her room, with her notebook and pen in hand, that she let it take her there.

The story that Devorah wrote was set — of all places — on the moon. She described a city that the people in her story built on the moon. They enclosed the city in a great, transparent bubble that allowed them to breathe and walk normally despite the moon's low gravity. When someone wanted to leave the city for whatever reason, he strapped himself into a smaller bubble that supplied him with air and propelled him to wherever he wished to go.

Devorah made up a fascinating tale of two boys who decided to go exploring in their bubbles. The story described their excitement as they planned the trip, their adventures along the way, and the mishaps that nearly led to their deaths. Long before they finally made it home to their moon-city, the boys had learned important lessons about friendship and responsibility and making the right choices.

It was a good story.

No, it was a *great* story!

Her heart in her mouth, Devorah handed it in to

her English teacher on the day before the deadline. It was as polished as she could make it. The rest was up to the judges — and Hashem.

And it was Hashem that Devorah thanked from the bottom of her heart when, just six weeks later, the contest results were announced. Devorah was the winner!

First prize was five hundred dollars and a *lot* of attention. Devorah was interviewed by a famous children's magazine, and a short piece appeared in the local newspaper, along with an excerpt from "Bubbles." Her school was bursting with pride. And the principal decided that, at the next assembly, Devorah would stand up and read her story aloud to the entire school.

Which was exactly what Devorah was doing now. And loving every minute of it.

She was surrounded by warmth and acclaim. Her family was proud of her. Her school was proud of her. She was up on stage, sharing the words that had emerged from her imagination and been crafted by her skill, and her fellow students were devouring every word. Their silence was the biggest tribute they could pay to Devorah's talent.

It was, without a doubt, the best day of her life.

"Ho, hum," Naomi said as they sauntered along after school. "What a boring day. I hate the middle of the winter, don't you? It's like one long stretch of *blah*."

Devorah, who'd been reliving those wonderful moments onstage, shook off the memory and stared at her friend. "What are you talking about, Naomi? I think this was the most exciting day in the world!"

Naomi gave her a sour look. "For you, maybe. But it's over now. What do we have to look forward to? Just tests and homework, and more tests and more homework. *Blah!*"

"Oh, I don't know," Devorah said dreamily. "There are so many more stories I want to write. They're dancing around in my head, just waiting for me to put them into words."

"Well, goody for you," Naomi snapped.

Devorah was startled out of her pleasant reverie. "Hey, what's the matter? You sound weird."

Her friend hesitated. Then, as if the words were being pushed out of her in a tidal wave that had been building up for a long time, she burst out, "Bubbles! That's what *you* live in, Devorah. A bubble!"

"What are you talking about?"

"I'm talking about the way you're never really *with* me. You're always off in some other place — a place inside your own head. A place that's not even *real*! You live inside a bubble, and no one else can get in …"

Devorah was stunned — and confused. A thousand different feelings tumbled around in her heart, making it hard to figure out the right way to respond to her friend's outburst.

But before she could even think of an answer, Naomi broke into a run. She sprinted ahead of Devorah, down the block, and across the street.

Devorah could have run after her. Maybe she could have caught her before Naomi reached her house. Maybe she could have demanded that her friend talk the whole thing over.

But she was too shaken up to react until it was too late. Naomi had vanished in a cloud of dust, and Devorah was alone.

The best day of her life had just turned into the worst. The very air she breathed tasted dry as moon-dust ....

Devorah was a girl who generally kept her feelings to herself, but it wasn't hard for her mother to see that her spirits were low as she came through the front door. Which was very strange, considering that she'd left the house in the highest of spirits that morning.

"Hi, Devorah. How'd the story reading go?"

"It was great," Devorah said dully. She dumped her knapsack on the floor and sank into an armchair.

"*You* don't sound so great," Ma remarked, a question in her voice.

To her astonishment — and dismay — her daughter burst into tears.

"I don't get it, Ma!" Devorah sobbed. "A best friend is supposed to be happy for you, isn't she?"

"Of course." Ma waited.

"Naomi's not happy for me," Devorah said softly, gazing at her mother with pain-filled eyes. "She's angry at me."

"What's she angry about?"

"She said ..." Devorah gulped. "She said that I live in a bubble, just like in my story, only the bubble is my own imagination. She said I'm never really w-with *her* ...." She was sobbing again.

Ma held her and soothed her until she could talk again. "I c-can't be different! This is who I am!" Devorah cried in despair. "I can't promise Naomi that I'll never daydream again." Her shoulders slumped sadly. "I was s-so happy that she wanted to be my friend ... But I guess that's over now." She heaved a long, shuddering sigh.

"Not necessarily," Ma said. "Listen to me, Devorah. Everyone lives inside his own private bubble. No one can ever really get inside another person's head. But you know what happens when two bubbles meet?"

Her daughter looked at her, eyes wide and damp.

"They hook up! They become one bigger bubble." Ma squeezed her shoulders and stood up. "You think about that, sweetie. I have to fix dinner before your brothers get home."

Devorah did think about it. And even though she

thought she knew what her mother meant, she didn't see how it was going to help her deal with Naomi.

Devorah had a fantastic imagination — but, try as she might, she couldn't imagine anything she might say that would bring her best friend back.

She spent a restless night caught up in gloomy dreams, tossing and turning until her blankets were in a huge tangle. When she awoke, the outlook was no less gloomy. She would walk to school as usual, but she had no idea what she would find when she got there. Would Naomi give her the cold shoulder? Would she explain yesterday's outburst?

Would she ever want to talk to her again?

"Bye, Ma." She tried to muster a smile as she slipped her lunch bag into her knapsack and started for the door.

"Good-bye, Devorah," her mother called after her. "And good luck ..."

"Thanks." As she trudged through a couple of inches of fresh snow, she pictured herself moving inside a bubble, like the people in her story. Maybe Naomi was right. Maybe Devorah was simply not fit to be anyone's friend. Maybe the only thing she was fit for was writing stories about friendship.

"Hey!" The soft call came from behind her right shoulder.

Devorah jumped. "Who …?" She turned around. It was Naomi.

"What are you doing here?" Devorah gasped. Her heart was beating way too fast. "This block is not even on your way to school."

"I know. I took a little detour, hoping I'd get to see you."

Devorah turned back around and began walking again. "Well, here I am." She wondered if Naomi had come here to continue the criticism she'd started dishing out the day before.

Naomi fell into step beside her. "Look, I want to apologize. I shouldn't have said that stuff to you yesterday."

"Why not? If it's true …"

"It may be true that you're off in your own world a lot," Naomi said. "But … there are other things that are just as true." The words seemed to be sticking in her throat.

"Like what?"

"Like … how jealous I am of you."

Devorah came to a standstill. She stared at Naomi. "You — jealous of *me*? What in the world for?" She was a loser who lived in a bubble inside her own head. She couldn't even manage to hold onto her first and only best friend. Naomi … jealous?

"Of your talent, of course. And the way you don't seem to care what other people think of you. You have such a rich life inside your mind that you don't really *have* to care!"

"I care about what *you* think of me," Devorah said shyly. Now it was *her* words that were getting stuck in her throat. Slowly, the two girls started walking again.

"Why? I'm a nothing. A jealous, resentful nothing who talks too much and hurts people's feelings." Naomi seemed determined to beat herself up this morning. She slanted a look at Devorah. "Come on, admit it. You were hurt by what I said yesterday, weren't you?"

"Of course," Devorah said simply.

"Well, like I said — I'm sorry. And now, if you want, I'll leave you alone." Naomi started to walk faster, as if she intended to leave Devorah behind again in the dust ... or rather, in the snow. Up ahead, the school building loomed into view.

"But I *don't* want."

Devorah's words were not loud, but they stopped Naomi in her tracks.

"Look," Devorah continued. "In a way, everyone lives inside a bubble. My mother says that no one can ever really know what's inside another person's head. But that doesn't mean that we can't ... well, float along together. Know what I mean?"

Naomi knew what Devorah meant. Devorah would have her daydreams, and Naomi would have her jealousy. And maybe, as they floated along together, they could find a way to help each other function a little better. Naomi could help Devorah live a little more outside her own head … and Devorah could help Naomi start liking who she was, so that she wouldn't have to envy other people.

Naomi nodded. She seemed suddenly shy, too.

"So … let's float."

Devorah grinned. Then she checked her watch.

"Yikes! Forget about floating — let's run! We're late!"

And the two girls made a mad dash for the school building — two lonely bubbles whose hearts had touched for a moment, to form one big, iridescent bubble of happiness.

SNEAK ATTACK

I t was a perfect spring day.

The sun shone just strongly enough, but not *too* strongly. In the grassy, tree-lined lot where the boys were playing ball, the air was filled with the chirping of hidden birds and the rustling of emerald leaves. Here and there, bees droned in the wildflowers. The only other sounds were the pleasant ones of boys' voices calling out to each other in the excitement of the game.

Suddenly, the pleasant cries were replaced by a loud, angry shout.

"You're OUT!" Yoni yelled.

"I am not!" cried the runner from the opposing

team. "I touched the base before you caught the ball. I'm safe!"

This being an informal baseball game, there was no umpire around to issue a ruling. The two boys continued to argue, with Yoni's voice getting louder and his face redder with each passing second.

"YOU ... ARE ... OUT!" Yoni insisted heatedly. "I saw exactly where your foot was when I caught the ball. And it was nowhere *near* the base!"

"Not true! I am *definitely* safe. Ask anyone!"

Of course, by this time every member of both teams had run over, waving their arms and shouting their opinions. But no one shouted louder than Yoni.

"This is so UNFAIR!" he bellowed. "I can't BELIEVE you guys! Mendy was one hundred percent OUT!"

"No way. He's safe!" the other team yelled back.

Yoni threw down his glove in disgust. "If you guys are gonna cheat, them I'm out of here!" His face was a mask of fury as he scooped up his glove and stomped out of the lot. One or two of his friends started after him, but others told them not to bother. They knew that when Yoni got mad, there was no point in arguing with him.

Yoni's anger stuck with him all the way home. Over and over, he reviewed the last play. He saw Mendy sprinting for first base. He saw the infielder tossing the ball to Yoni, the first baseman. He heard the satisfying *smack!* as the ball landed in his glove, and then the thump of Mendy's sneakered foot hitting the base. Mendy had absolutely come *after* the ball. He was out!

"Those guys cheated," Yoni growled to himself. If there was one thing Yoni hated, it was injustice. It made him feel as if the world had tilted at a crazy angle and was teetering on its axis, off-balance. And it made him see red.

"Hi, Yoni," his mother greeted him as he came through the front door, slamming it shut behind him. Then she noticed his face, which looked like a raincloud about to burst. "What's the matter?"

"Those guys!" Yoni burst out. "They said Mendy was safe when he was absolutely, one hundred percent OUT! I tried to tell them, but would they listen? I am SO fed up with them!"

His mother soothed him as best she could, but she was worried. Whether or not Mendy was safe was beside the point. What troubled Ma was the way Yoni had reacted. The way he *always* reacted. Yoni had a hot temper, and it worried both his parents.

By dinnertime, Yoni had calmed down, with the help of an ice-cold glass of lemonade and a fun game of cards with his brother Tully. Right *after* dinner, though, it was Tully who made Yoni's face turn red all over again.

"I'm going over to Berel's house to study for our test, Ma," Tully called on his way to the door. Berel, his best friend, lived right around the corner.

"Okay. Good luck with your studying," Ma called back.

In a flash, Yoni was at the front door, blocking Tully's way. "Oh, no, you don't. You're supposed to do the dishes tonight, remember?"

"But Sunday's *your* night!" Tully protested.

"I took your turn last week, remember? And you said you'd take *my* turn tonight."

"But I have to go study. Berel's waiting for me!"

"The DISHES are waiting for you!"

"I'll do them tomorrow," Tully said, trying to slip past him.

"YOU'LL DO THEM TONIGHT!" Yoni yelled.

Their father came out of his study. "What's all the shouting about, boys?"

"It's Tully's turn to do the dishes, and he's trying to weasel out of it!"

Daddy lifted a questioning brow. "Tully?"

"Yoni took my turn last week, so I owe him one. But I can do it another night. I have to go study now."

"This is SO UNFAIR!" Yoni yelled. "I was COUNTING on him to do the dishes TONIGHT!"

"Maybe he can take your next turn?" his father asked. Pointedly, he added, "And maybe you can discuss this without shouting the house down ..."

"Tully *always* finds a way to get out of doing his job!" Yoni muttered, his face still red but his voice a decibel or two lower.

"Bye, everyone. See you later …." Tully escaped out the front door.

Yoni was about to stomp off to his room when his father stopped him. "Yoni, I meant what I said just now. You lose your temper far too often. It's not a good *middah*, to say the least."

"Sorry, Daddy … But it gets me so mad! First the ball game today, and now this. I *hate* when things aren't fair!"

"Nobody likes injustice, Yoni. But you have to work on responding calmly."

Yoni swallowed, as though trying to gulp down his anger. "I'll try …."

And Yoni did try. He tried all the rest of that night, and the next morning. Luckily, he didn't have to try very hard, because nothing came along to push his buttons … until recess.

Now that the days had turned warmer, there was always a scramble at recess to be the first one in the school yard. The first boys to reach the yard got to stake out a nice, big area where they could play ball, while everyone else was forced to make do with more cramped quarters along the sides of the yard.

Yoni loved playing ball, and he was a fast runner. So today, he'd decided to dash outside the instant the bell rang, to claim the best ball-playing spot.

He did it. Before the bell had even stopped ringing, he was out of the classroom and halfway down the stairs. Behind him, he heard the noise of his fellow students stampeding out for recess, but he was ahead of them all. He staked out the playing field by standing right in the middle of it, arms crossed triumphantly across his chest.

As he stood waiting for his friends to join him, a teacher came hurrying over.

"I need you to give a message to the office," Mr. Stein told Yoni breathlessly.

"But I —"

"It's urgent. Please tell the principal that I just got word of a family emergency and must rush home. He needs to send another teacher out here for recess duty right away!"

At that moment, three boys came running up to where Yoni stood. They were not in his grade. "This spot is taken?" one of them asked, disappointed.

"Yes." Yoni shot a look at Mr. Stein, who waved an anxious hand to hurry him along. "It's *my* spot. I'll be right back!"

He couldn't delay any longer. Yoni ran pell-mell for the school building, yelling over his shoulder at the boys, "My friends will be here any second!"

Yoni reached the office at record speed and delivered Mr. Stein's message to Rabbi Singer, the principal. Then he spun around and began sprinting back the way he'd come.

The yard was crowded now. Everywhere he

looked, boys were milling around, tossing balls, eating snacks. He headed straight for the spot he'd claimed.

To his dismay — and fury — he found the three boys he'd spoken to earlier, along with a bunch of their friends. They were playing ball on HIS spot!

"Hey! I was here first!" Yoni said indignantly.

One of the other boys shrugged. "You left. We took over. That's all."

"That is NOT all!" Yoni's face was growing dangerously red again. "This is SO UNFAIR! I *told* you I'd be right back!" He stopped as a question struck him. "My friends — where are they?"

The boy shrugged again. "Somewhere else ... obviously." His pals laughed.

Yoni had never felt less like laughing in his life. He'd run like the wind to capture this spot. "*You'd* better go somewhere else!" he bellowed. "I WAS HERE FIRST!"

His shouts attracted a lot of attention — including that of his friends, who'd started a modest game in a corner of the yard. They came running over and managed, with difficulty, to drag Yoni away, yelling as he went.

"I can't BELIEVE those guys! I TOLD them it was our spot! And then they went and STOLE it!" The whole world seemed to rock with the injustice of it.

"That's the way it goes," his friend Moshe said philosophically. "C'mon, Yoni. Let's play some ball before recess is over."

But Yoni was too upset to play. He sat out the game, glaring at the usurpers playing ball in "his" spot, until the bell rang again.

Yoni was busy doing homework in his room that night when he heard the phone ring downstairs.

Through the half-open door, he was dimly aware of his father's voice talking to someone. Afterwards, there was a short silence. Then, "Yoni!"

Yoni lifted his head. "I'm up here, Daddy!" He got to his feet. But his father was up the stairs and in his room before Yoni had even reached the door.

"Sit down," his father said. "We have to talk."

Uh-oh. Yoni sat back down.

"That was Rabbi Singer on the phone just now."

"My p-principal?"

"Exactly. And do you know what he wanted to talk to me about?"

Yoni shook his head.

"Do you remember a certain incident at recess to-day?"

Yoni sat up. "You won't *believe* what happened, Daddy! I ran ahead of everyone to reserve the best spot for a ball game — and then these guys *stole* it from me. Just because a teacher asked me to take a message to the office! How unfair is that?"

"Not very fair at all," Daddy agreed. "But Rabbi

Singer says you expressed yourself with anger." He paused. "A *lot* of anger."

"Of course I was angry! Wouldn't you have been?"

His father leaned forward. He looked very serious. "Here's the thing, Yoni. There are three parts to this problem. One" — he counted on his fingers — "something happens that you find unjust. Two, you get mad. And, three, you act out of that anger. Does that sound about right?"

Yoni nodded. That was exactly the way it always happened.

"Now, here's where the *yetzer hara* steps in," his father continued. "He takes something real — a genuine injustice — and helps rile you up so that you're good and mad about it. And then he urges you to start *acting* mad. Yelling, turning red, and so on ... See the picture?"

Yoni wasn't sure.

"It's like a sneak attack," Daddy explained. "The *yetzer hara* sneaks up behind you, so to speak, while you're dealing with a situation that you feel is wrong and unfair. And then, before you know it, you're doing the wrong thing!"

"But —"

"Hear me out, Yoni. This is important. You have to be on guard all the time. Because the *yetzer hara* doesn't try to convince you to do an outright *aveirah, chas v'shalom.* He's cleverer than that. Instead, he tells you, 'You're so right, Yoni. This *is* unfair. This *is* unjust. *They're* wrong — and *you're* right!' And then he gives you permission to act any way you please. Even in ways that are very improper."

Yoni thought about this. He hung his head. "I guess I did yell a bit in the school yard today ...."

"*And* at your brother last night ..."

"And at the ball game yesterday afternoon. I was positive that Mendy was out, but everyone else said he was safe."

His father gave him an encouraging smile. "Just remember to keep your eyes peeled for that old *yetzer hara*. Don't let him talk you into forgetting your good *middos* ... even when you're busy fighting injustice!"

Yoni went to sleep that night determined to get the better of that wily old *yetzer hara*. He would look over his shoulder — so to speak — every second of the day.

As the days went by, Yoni sometimes succeeded with flying colors. He caught the sound of the little voice whispering in his ear, "It's okay to lose your temper this time. This is *really* unfair!" Those times, he noticed the danger before it was too late.

Other times, he failed. But he kept on trying.

His father had told him that the best way to know you've done genuine *teshuvah* is if you're in the same place, facing the same situation — and you do the right thing instead of the wrong one.

It wasn't until another Sunday, toward the tail end of summer, that Yoni finally felt as if he might be making progress.

It was another ball game, in the same grassy, tree-ringed lot, with the same birds and breeze and bees and kids.

Yoni hit the ball and watched it sail into the sky. Dropping the bat, he began a mad dash for first base.

Someone scooped up the ball and threw it at the first baseman, who caught it just as Yoni was sliding into first.

"OUT!" called the first baseman.

"No way! I'm *safe!*" Yoni gasped.

Instantly, everyone started running over and voicing his opinion.

"Out!"

"Safe!"

Yoni was positive that he'd been safe. Most of the other kids seemed to feel otherwise.

Yoni felt a surge of anger rising up inside. *This is SO unfair!* he thought.

The urgent voice of the *yetzer hara* began telling him that he was one hundred percent correct. That it was okay to lose his temper like he'd never lost it before. That it would serve that first baseman right to be blasted right off the planet!

The trap lay in front of him, doubly dangerous because it was so cleverly hidden. Yoni was in danger of sliding right in ….

And then he remembered.

Instead of blowing off steam, he put up his safety guard.

Instead of letting the anger take over, he closed his mouth. Tight.

He wouldn't say a word — even if he was convinced that he was right.

So Yoni was out.

And Yoni was safe.

WISE
EYES

"Nice glasses," Yossi remarked, as he and Yanky walked home from school. "Are they new?"

Yanky nodded. "My old ones broke."

"I can't imagine needing glasses," Yossi confided. "I've never had to wear them."

"Oh, they're not so bad. They keep me from bumping into things …."

Actually, Yanky was a little sensitive about his glasses. He was one of the few boys in his class who had to wear them, and he secretly thought they made him look even nerdier than he was. It was bad enough that he couldn't tell one end of a baseball bat from the other! With his glasses on, he thought he looked like a solemn old man.

Yossi was not the most perceptive of boys, but even he could tell that his friend wanted to talk about something else. Obligingly, he dropped the subject of glasses and started talking about sports, which, in Yanky's opinion, was not much better. He was relieved when they reached Yossi's house. A cold drink and a board game would go a long way toward lifting his spirits.

It was not to be. Hardly had the two boys set foot in the house, when they spotted a white envelope with a big, black "C" scrawled across the outside.

"Mr. Chesed needs us!" Yossi cried. "Let's go!"

Dropping their knapsacks in the hall, the boys sprinted back outside and down the block. In no time at all, they saw the familiar red, yellow, and blue sign at the edge of a quiet, dead-end street. The sign read "CHESED CARNIVAL."

Mr. Chesed was waiting to give them their next mission. Where would he send them this time?

"New glasses?" Mr. Chesed asked, after he'd greeted the boys with his usual warm smile.

Yanky nodded. He didn't want to talk about his glasses. He was eager to be off on their mission!

"Nice." There was a mysterious twinkle in Mr. Chesed's eyes as he escorted his guests out to where the Chesed Roller Coaster lay waiting in the sun. "I think they'll come in handy where you're going ...."

"Where *are* we going?" Yossi asked eagerly.

But — as usual — Mr. Chesed didn't answer. He only said, "Buckle up tight, boys. Have a safe trip!"

The boys buckled up. Yossi pressed the starter switch. They were off!

After a journey of mind-blurring speed, they found themselves on a hilltop overlooking a large city. The roller coaster parked behind some concealing trees. The boys hopped out.

"Looks like a big place," Yossi said, peering at the sprawling city. "Where do we start?"

"At the beginning," Yanky replied cheerfully. He was always happy at the start of a new mission. "Let's just start walking. Something's bound to turn up. It always does."

They started walking — down the hill, across a short meadow, and onto a blacktop road that led to the first, straggling houses on the outskirts of the city.

It was near one of these houses — a pleasant, if slightly rundown place, two stories tall with a flowering magnolia tree out front — that Yanky stumbled on a hidden rock. A sharp pain shot through his ankle as he fell. When he tried to stand up again, he found that he couldn't.

He was chagrined. Here they were, hardly twenty minutes into their mission, and he had to go and hurt himself!

"I can't walk," he gasped. "Can you ask for help

at that house? Maybe if my ankle was bandaged up, I could hobble around." Not likely. With each passing second, his ankle was swelling — and hurting more. But how could he tell Yossi that their mission was over even before it had started?

Yossi had to knock twice before someone opened the door. A little boy with a mop of curly brown hair and woebegone eyes stood there.

"Can I speak to your mother?" Yossi asked politely. "My friend here" — he gestured at Yanky, who was sitting on a rock at the end of the path — "hurt his foot. We need a bandage or something."

"My mommy's not alive anymore," the little boy told him with a sniffle. "Do you want to talk to my daddy?"

"Uh, sure," Yossi said uncomfortably. "I'm sorry about your mother. When did it happen?"

"When I was five-and-a-half," the boy said. "I'm six now."

Pity welled up in Yossi's heart as he watched the boy trot away toward the back of the house. From what he could see of the house, the place could have used a mother's touch. While it was spotlessly clean, there was none of the cozy clutter that turns a house into a home ....

"Yes?"

Startled, Yossi realized that the boy had returned, leading a tall man with pale-blue eyes. Right now, those eyes were regarding him with some impatience.

"I'm a little busy at the moment, young man ...."

"My friend injured his foot," Yossi said. "His ankle's really hurting him. Could we have some ice, and maybe a bandage?"

Instantly, the man softened. "I'll do better than that. I'll get my next-door neighbor, Dr. Morton, to have a look at him. How's that?"

"Thanks!" Yossi beamed. "I really appreciate it, sir."

His host was probably regretting his offer when, half an hour later, the doctor finished his examination and straightened up from the couch where Yanky was lying.

"It's a bad sprain," he announced. "I'm going to bandage it now, but you'll have to stay off that foot for at least a few days, to let it heal."

"A few days?" Yanky repeated in dismay.

"A few *days*?" His host seemed even more dismayed.

"A few days," the doctor said firmly. He stood up and picked up his bag. "I'll be back to check it tomorrow. Stay off that foot, young man!"

When Dr. Morton had left, Yanky and Yossi looked at their host, who looked back at them with a rather helpless expression. "You could stay in the guest room," he said.

His children — an older brother and sister had joined the six-year-old — visibly brightened.

"Yes!" said Marty, who appeared to be about eleven.

"I'll go make sure the room's ready," said Sarah, the nine-year-old daughter.

And Sam, the little boy who'd opened the door for Yossi, volunteered: "Mommy used to put flowers in the guest room when we had someone staying there."

"Why don't you go pick some, then?" his sister suggested. As her little brother trotted out to the garden, she whispered to Yossi and Yanky, "Sam's been so sad since our mother died last year. He hardly ever smiles anymore ...."

She didn't seem to be smiling much, either. And her older brother looked none too cheerful himself. There was no question about it: This was a sad house.

Yossi and Yanky exchanged a glance. How could they help?

It was after supper (Yossi and Yanky had requested raw fruits and vegetables for their "special diet") when they first saw the glasses.

Mr. Simms, their host, stood up from the table and said, "Well, I'll be in the library if anyone needs me." As he walked away, he pulled a case from his pocket. He opened it and put on the glasses that lay inside.

"We won't see him again till the morning," Sarah sighed.

She and Marty began silently clearing the table. Yossi helped, while Yanky watched from the couch where he rested with his bandaged foot elevated. Young Sam sat staring out the window.

Yossi was curious. "What does your father do in the library all evening?"

"He sees things," Sarah said.

"Far-away things," Marty added.

"With his glasses," Sam chimed in.

Under the boys' coaxing, the children told them about the marvelous glasses. Only the very rich or the very educated could get hold of a pair. Mr. Simms belonged to the latter group. When he wore the glasses, he could see things that were far away. He could watch scientists in their laboratories and observe natural phenomena many miles distant. He could study the stars and inspect the bottom of the sea. He could see the whole world!

The problem was, when he had his glasses on Mr. Simms lost all track of time. He forgot where he was and what was going on around him. Sometimes, in the mornings, the children would find him asleep in his chair in the library. He'd been so enthralled by his studies that he never even made it upstairs to bed.

"With his glasses, Father can see everything," Marty said with a sigh.

What he *couldn't* see, apparently, were the things that were happening right under his nose ....

Marty came home from school the next afternoon with a torn shirt and a graze on his cheek.

"What happened?" Yossi asked in dismay.

"Nothing ..."

"It's obviously not 'nothing.' C'mon, Marty! What's going on?"

"There's this bully at school," Marty muttered. "He's always starting up with me."

"Well, why don't you tell your father? He could speak to the principal."

Marty answered with a roll of his eyes.

Marty wasn't the only one. Later, through the open window near the couch where Yanky sat propped up on some cushions, he heard someone sobbing in the bushes. A few minutes later, Sarah returned to the house, red-eyed and listless. Yanky called out to her. Reluctantly, she shuffled over to the couch, staring at the floor.

"Sarah, I heard you crying just now," Yanky said quietly. "Why don't you tell me about it? Maybe I can help."

"Nobody can help," Sarah whimpered.

"Try me."

Sarah hesitated, but the pain inside her was too big to stay inside.

"Elsie ... my best friend, just d-dumped me ...."

"Why'd she do a thing like that?"

"She has a d-different best friend no-o-ow ...." The sentence ended with a wail.

"I'm sorry, Sarah. That must hurt. Did you tell your father?" It was a parent's job to console his child at a time like this.

Sarah shook her head. "He's got his glasses on. When he's wearing his glasses, he doesn't p-pay attention to anybody ...."

First Marty, and now Sarah. Yossi and Yanky were distressed for the brother and sister who had no one to guide and console them — or, at least, no one who seemed willing to do the job. As for young Sam, it didn't take a genius to figure out what was the matter with *him*. He missed his mommy terribly. Sarah confided to Yanky that Sam cried himself to sleep every night.

"Does your father know?" Yanky asked, his heart aching for the little boy.

Sarah didn't even bothering answering that one.

Yanky made up his mind: Something had to be done.

And he would be the one to do it.

"Your children told me about your incredible glasses," Yanky told Mr. Simms before dinner that night. *After* the meal, he knew, the man would disappear into his library and not be seen again until the morning.

His host smiled happily. "Yes, the glasses *are* incredible. They impart such wisdom! When I wear them, I can see everything there is to see. I can study without end! My colleagues and I can pinpoint trouble spots in the world and correct problems before they grow bigger. We can discover new forms of plant and animal life. These glasses help us unlock the secrets of the universe!"

"Impressive," Yanky said. "As you may have noticed," he added, "I wear glasses, too."

"Are your glasses special, like mine?"

Yanky nodded solemnly. "Very special. They can see things that are hidden."

"Such as what?" Mr. Simms asked eagerly.

"Such as ... the secrets of the human heart."

His host looked confused. "What do you mean?"

"When I wear these glasses, I can see the pain in a boy's heart when he goes to school afraid of being bullied — again. I can see the tears in a girl's heart when her best friend abandons her. And I can see the sorrow in a little boy's heart, when he misses his mother so much that he cries himself to sleep every night ...."

Mr. Simms stared at him. "You can't be talking about ..." He cleared his throat. "... about *my* children. Can you?"

"I can, sir. And I *am*."

"But ... but ..."

Yanky waited.

"But why haven't they said anything to me? I would have tried to help them."

"With respect, sir, you're too busy studying the world. You're busy looking at things that are far away. But there are important things for you to see — *right here*."

There was a short silence.

"With my glasses," Mr. Simms whispered, "I can spot problems across the world. I can help fix them ...."

Yanky gave him a very direct look. "Where I come from, we have a saying: 'Charity begins at home' ...."

He looked at Mr. Simms, who looked utterly stricken. It didn't take a pair of special glasses to tell him that his host had gotten the message.

"Good-bye! Good-bye!" The father and his three children stood in the doorway, waving.

Yanky — walking carefully on his newly healed foot — turned around for one last glimpse of the family.

You couldn't exactly call them a happy family yet. But you could see the seeds of future happiness in the way they stood. Mr. Simms was holding little Sam's hand, while Sarah and Marty crowded close around them.

Of the amazing glasses that could see to the ends of the earth, there was no sign. Right now, Mr. Simms had more important things to look at. Like his children's faces. And his children's hearts …

Yanky turned to Yossi, who was waiting to hike back to the Chesed Roller Coaster. "Mission accomplished!" He'd never pronounced those two words with quite the same sense of satisfaction.

"That was a good one," Yossi said, with the same sense of accomplishment.

Yanky hesitated. "Tell me the truth, Yossi. Do my glasses make me look nerdy?"

Yossi considered him. "I think they make you look smart."

"Really?"

"Sure."

Yanky grinned and pushed his glasses higher up on the bridge of his nose. Of course, it *was* possible to look smart and nerdy at the same time — but he wouldn't let that thought bother him right now. He was feeling too good.

"C'mon, Yossi," he cried. "Let's go home!"

SCATTERBRAIN

Here's the thing about my sister: She's terribly scatterbrained.

Everyone knows it. Toby's teachers complain about all the assignments she simply forgets to do. Her siblings (mainly, me!) feel like tearing their hair out when she forgets to give them important phone messages — like the time I missed out on a great babysitting job because Toby carefully wrote down the information but then forgot to give me the note.

Our mother probably suffers the most from Toby's absent-mindedness. She's always having to check and double-check that Toby got things right. Sometimes I feel like Ma ought to hire a full-time secretary to go around with Toby and make sure she stays on top of things.

Instead, that job usually falls on me. Though I'm a year younger than my sister, I'm the one who ends up organizing her knapsack and reminding her to get her tests signed. To be honest, I don't really mind. I'm naturally neat and organized, so it's kind of fun making order for Toby. I only wish I could make some order inside that scattered mind of hers!

Take last night, for example. I was passing through the kitchen when I saw her at the counter. Baking ingredients were laid out in front of her and she was pouring chocolate-cake batter into a pan. Toby and her friends like to give each other cakes on their birthdays. She would probably decorate it with sprinkles and take it to school with her in the morning.

"So who's this one for?" I asked, as Toby pulled open the oven door. She was about to insert the pan when I added, "Don't you have to preheat the oven first?"

My sister glanced at the indicator light. It wasn't on. "You're right," she groaned. "Cakes always come out better when the oven is preheated." She put down the pan of batter, turned on the oven to the right temperature, and sat down to wait. "Thanks, Elisheva."

"No problem." I hesitated. There was a speech quivering on the tip of my tongue. A speech about getting her act together. About learning to be more methodical and less scatterbrained ...

But in the end I said nothing. What was the use? I'd already given my sister a thousand such speeches. Toby was Toby, and that was that.

"Toby, can you come here a minute?" Ma called from the living room on the following afternoon. We had just come home from school to find our little brother, Shaya, lying on the couch looking perfectly miserable. Ma was seated beside him, a cool hand on his forehead.

Toby dumped her knapsack and approached the couch. "What's wrong with Shaya?"

"He's running a fever. If he's not better by the morning, I'll take him to the doctor. But right now, I have a favor to ask you."

"Sure, Ma. What is it?"

"I need you to pick up a few things at the grocery. I meant to run out earlier, but then Shaya wasn't feeling well." Ma reached into her apron pocket. "Here's the list. You can pick up all these things at Stein's grocery store. There's no need to hike all the way over to the supermarket. If you'll bring me my pocketbook, I'll give you a debit card to use when you pay."

Toby nodded absently as she folded the list into quarters and shoved it into the pocket of her jacket, which she hadn't even taken off yet. "I'll go right now."

She was halfway to the door when Ma called, "Aren't you forgetting something?"

My sister paused, a hand on the doorknob. "Um ... I have the list ...."

"What about paying for the things you buy?"

"Oh, right! The debit card." Toby trotted over to the front closet, where Ma keeps her pocketbook. In a minute, Ma found the card she wanted and handed it to Toby, who put it in her pocket along with the list.

"I'm on my way," she said cheerfully, and started for the door again.

The door closed behind her, letting in a blast of chilly air. Hardly five seconds had passed before the door opened up again. Toby poked her head inside. "You said the supermarket, right?"

Ma sighed with frustration. "I said you *don't* have to go all the way to the supermarket, Toby. I said you could pick up the things at Stein's Grocery, around the corner!"

"Oh, that's right. I remember now ... Well, bye!" And, with a wave, she was gone again.

And that, in a nutshell, is Toby.

I wasn't there, of course, but I can tell you exactly what happened to my sister at Stein's Grocery. I know because of what happened afterwards.

Toby went around the corner to the store and

picked up a basket to hold the things she was going to buy. Her hand went into her pocket to find the list that Ma had given her.

Now, you have to understand something about Toby's pockets. She puts everything in them. At any given time of the day or night, you can find an assortment of strange and sometimes inexplicable items in her pocket. Things like unusually-shaped stones, bent-out-of-shape paper clips, a tiny screwdriver for fixing glasses, sucking candies — both wrapped and unwrapped — and the odd nickel or two. I once even saw her take out a brand-new baby shoe!

When I asked her why she was carrying around the tiny shoe, she said she'd found it on our block and was planning to knock on the neighbors' doors to find out if anyone had lost it. (The shoe turned out to belong to little Esti Davis, down the street. And her mother was overjoyed to have it back!)

But back to our story. Toby reached into her pocket and felt around among the jumble of things in there, until she pulled out the piece of paper with Ma's list. One by one, she plucked the items on the list off the shelves and put them in her basket. When she'd collected everything, she went to the counter to pay. That done, she left the grocery store and started for home, proud of herself for having done such a good job with the shopping.

When she arrived, I'd taken Ma's place on the

couch with Shaya while Ma was in the kitchen finishing the supper preparations. Toby lugged the shopping bag into the kitchen and put it on the table. I heard Ma thank her. There was a short silence, except for a rustle as Ma started going through the things in the bag.

The kitchen door was wide open, which was how I heard what came next.

"Toby," Ma said in a strange voice. "What are these things?"

"What things?"

"The things you bought."

"They're the things on the list."

Curious, I got up. I reached the kitchen door just in time to see my mother close her eyes. Then she opened them again and asked quietly, "Which list was that?"

"The one you gave me." After a few seconds of groping in that busy pocket, Toby pulled out a slip of folded paper. "Here!" she said triumphantly, and gave it to Ma.

Ma looked down at the list. "Toby," she said in a strangled voice. "This isn't the list I gave you today. This is an *old* list that I gave you a couple of weeks ago! You already bought all these things back then!"

"Oops," Toby said in a small voice. "I didn't notice."

"How did this happen? Don't you ever clean out your pockets?"

"Uh …"

"Don't answer that." Ma sighed. "Do you still have today's list?"

Once again, Toby fished around in her pocket. She finally pulled out a second piece of folded paper, identical to the first.

"Good," Ma said, glancing at it to make sure it was the right list. "Now, please take these things back to Mr. Stein. Tell him what happened, and then exchange all of these groceries for the ones on this list. And hurry — it's nearly suppertime."

Just then, the phone rang. I answered. It was our neighbor, Mrs. Newberg, wanting to know if we had any barley she could borrow. She could also use some onion powder, if we had some to spare. And two stalks of celery.

"My sister's just about to go to the grocery," I offered. "Maybe she could pick up those things for you."

"Perfect! I'll pay your mother back later. Can you put Toby on?"

I gave Toby the phone. "Barley, onion powder, celery," she muttered, over and over. Finally, she decided not to trust her memory and wrote down the items on the back of Ma's list. And off she went, back to the grocery store.

I happened to be at the window when Toby was on her way home later. I saw her run into our neighbor's house to give Mrs. Newberg her bag. I saw her run out again. And then two seconds later I saw Mrs.

Newburg come out of her house, shopping bag in hand, and start running after Toby.

"Toby!" she called. "You gave me the wrong bag! This one must be your mother's." She held up her bag and pointed to the celery leaves sticking out of the top of the one in Toby's hand. "I wanted the celery, remember?"

I shook my head, though there was no one to see me. Trust Toby to mix things up again. What a scatterbrain!

They traded bags, and then my sister was back at last. My father was home by now, too. Ma quickly put away the groceries and called us to the table.

"What about Mr. Shamberg?" Toby said anxiously. "He's supposed to be coming over for supper, remember?"

Before Ma could answer, the doorbell rang. Toby's face lit up. She ran to the door and threw it open.

"Mr. Shamberg! Come in," she invited. Taking slow, small steps, he did.

Mr. Shamberg is very old. His wife died just last year, and he's been walking around wearing a lost look ever since. Since his children live far away, Ma and Ta often invite him for Shabbos meals and an occasional supper, as do most of our neighbors. Toby led him to the dining room table and showed him where to sit.

"Thank you, Toby," Mr. Shamberg said, smiling at her. "You're a good girl."

Toby glowed. Most of the time, people are busy criticizing her for getting things wrong. I guess she enjoyed hearing something good for a change. She took her seat and offered to pour our guest a drink of water.

The meal was good. Ta chatted with Mr. Shamberg while we all ate our fill of my mother's delicious meatballs and spaghetti. We don't usually have dessert during the week, so we were all surprised when Toby jumped up and said, "Everyone, stay where you are. I'll bring in the dessert."

I noticed a puzzled look on Ma's face. What dessert?

To tell the truth, I was wondering the same thing.

The kitchen door swung open again, and there was Toby — holding up a beautifully decorated cake. I recognized it as the one she'd been baking the night before. The cake I'd thought she was planning to bring to school for a friend ...

"Happy birthday, Mr. Shamberg!" Toby cried. She walked over to our neighbor's side of the table and carefully placed the cake right in front of him. Leaning over, I saw the same words written across the top in thin blue icing. Ta grinned at Toby and started singing "Happy Birthday to You."

Mr. Shamberg looked as if he was about to cry. In fact, I think I actually saw some tears in his eyes. His cheeks got very pink and he had to clear his throat a few times before a word would come out.

"Thank you, Toby," he said, giving her a shaky

smile. "This is really special. But how did you know that today's my birthday?"

"You once told me the date," Toby said. "I remembered."

I stared at my scatterbrained sister. We all stared at her. Was this the same Toby who constantly forgot her homework? The girl who mixed things up as easily as breathing? The one who couldn't even go to the grocery store without making a mess of things?

I sat back, struck by a sudden thought. Maybe it wasn't that Toby was naturally forgetful. Maybe she only chose to remember things that were really important to her.

Things like a lonely old man's birthday. And baking him a beautiful cake, just to make him happy.

Here's the thing about my sister Toby: She's terribly scatterbrained. Most of the time.

And here's another thing about my sister Toby — something it's taken me much too long to figure out: She has a heart of gold.

All of the time!

TURNING BACK
THE CLOCK

Hi. My name is Levi Sanders, and I like beginnings. There's something so clean and new — so *hopeful* — about beginnings. No matter what's come before, a fresh start means that all the other stuff is behind you.

You might remember something you did. You certainly might regret it. But it's behind you. And in front of you is an endless white page, just waiting to be written on.

That's exactly how I felt one month ago, on Rosh Chodesh Elul.

My rebbi at day camp had been talking to us about Elul. About how special this month is, because Hashem is closer than ever — just waiting for us to reach out to Him. He said that it's a time to try our very hardest to get things right, because Rosh Hashanah is right around the corner and that's when the whole world gets judged.

I'd heard those things before, of course. Until this year, I have to admit, they usually went in one ear and out the other. But I'm twelve years old now, and looking my bar mitzvah in the eye. If I don't get the message this year, when will I ever?

So I listened to my rebbi, and I made a resolution: This Elul, I was going to get it right.

And when I say "right," I mean *right*! Anyone who knows me will tell you that Levi Sanders is no half-measures kind of guy. When I decide do something, I throw myself into it — head first, and all the way.

Which is why I made up my mind, that Erev Rosh Chodesh Elul, that I was going to spend the next month — that all-important month leading up to Rosh Hashanah — being absolutely perfect.

I started off strong. On the first morning of Elul, I jumped out of bed like a lion, washed *negel vasser,* and hurried through my morning routine so that I'd be in shul with plenty of time to spare before Shacharis. I'm sorry to have to admit that, most mornings, I'm still half asleep during davening, or else my mind is filled with a million and one things that have nothing to do with the words I'm saying.

Before I left, I was careful to speak respectfully to my mother and kindly to my sisters. Even when I discovered that four-year-old Chani had been using the contents of my pencil case to draw pictures on the blank pages in my loose-leaf, I held onto my temper. Not bad, Levi!

On that Rosh Chodesh Elul, I was ready with my *siddur* a full five minutes before davening started. I tried my best to concentrate on the words. And I really succeeded! Halfway through Shemoneh Esrei, I started congratulating myself on my *kavanah*. I'd done it! I'd focused my mind and heart on the words of *tefillah*. I was pretty proud of myself. I pictured myself doing the same thing again the next day. I wondered why I'd always thought it was so hard before. I …

I was taking three steps back. I had finished Shemoneh Esrei, without remembering a single word I'd said for the last five *brachos*.

A wave of heat rushed through me, filling me from head to toe. The heat came from shame, from disappointment, from frustration. I'd been so proud of myself … and I'd messed up again!

Obviously, getting it right in the month of Elul was harder than I'd thought it would be. I took a deep breath and started over again. I'd already ruined my perfect record for today — but tomorrow was the second day of Elul. I'd get it right then.

On the second day of Rosh Chodesh Elul, I actually managed to keep my mind on davening all the way through. And in day camp I managed to keep my mind on the Gemara we were learning. A couple of hours later, it was time for our first sports activity of the day.

As we walked out onto the playing field, my friend Gershy told me a funny story. The story was about a dumb thing that a kid in our bunk had done. I laughed heartily at my bunkmate's antics, while privately thinking that he wasn't very smart ... It wasn't until I'd stepped onto the sunny field that the realization hit me, clear as the sunlight: I'd just participated in the *aveirah* of *lashon hara*.

I ground my teeth. Why couldn't I keep my mind on what I was doing? Why was it so *hard* to get it right?

A perfect record this month seemed farther away than ever. As I went through the motions of playing ball, I decided that I'd been too ambitious. A perfect month was way too much to expect from myself.

A whole month was unrealistic. I would take it week by week instead.

Do you know what failure tastes like? Let me tell you, it's not delicious. It's the sour taste of being disappointed in yourself. It's the metallic taste of regret. You want to take that taste and spit it out, but it lingers on your tongue, making you wish with all your heart that you could turn back the clock, to the moment just before you failed ....

Day after day, I tried to get it right. I wanted just one perfect week, but I couldn't even get started! Everywhere I went, the *yetzer hara* was there before me, lying in wait to trip me up. You'd think that after all the practice I had stumbling over his outstretched leg, so to speak, I'd have learned to avoid it by now. But no — I tripped over it every time. I did it because the *yetzer hara* is a master of disguise! I didn't see that leg waiting to trip me, for a very simple reason: Each time, the leg looked different.

Sometimes it looked like a fantastic story — one that I didn't realize concealed a hornet's nest of *lashon hara* until it was too late. Other times, it was an irresistible thought during davening, or an empty stomach that had me mumble a hasty, thoughtless *brachah* before taking my first bite. That *yetzer hara*'s leg looked different on every occasion — and it got me every time.

Finally, I woke up one morning and realized, to my shock, that Rosh Hashanah was only a week away. Something had to be done — and fast!

I hadn't managed a perfect record for the whole month of Elul. I hadn't even managed one perfect week.

"One day," I told myself as I stared up at the unsympathetic ceiling. "Just one perfect day. That's all I want." If I could get it right for one whole day — just one! — I'd feel like I was ready to greet Rosh Hashanah properly. I'd be able to hold up my head instead of hanging it down in failure.

One day. That's not too much to ask, is it?

Let me tell you, it was much harder than it sounds.

Each morning, I'd jump out of bed prepared to conquer the day. I'd go off to school filled with great intentions. And inevitably, by midday, or mid-afternoon — sometimes even by mid-morning — I'd mess up. My perfect record would be ruined. With a sigh, privately kicking myself, I'd decide to start over again the next day.

Finally, it was the last day. Tomorrow was Erev Rosh Hashanah.

I started out hopefully: on my best behavior in the house that morning, a good davening, learning well in class, saying my *brachos* with *kavanah* at lunch. I got all the way through the school day with my slate clean, as the saying goes. Back home again, I stayed in my room so I wouldn't be tempted to say or do anything wrong. At dinner, I ate quietly and then rushed upstairs to do my homework. Sara, my oldest sister, asked me if I was coming down with something, and Dina made a humorous crack at my expense, but I didn't respond. I was determined to get it right.

It was almost over. All I had to do was *daven* Maariv, and then I could crawl into bed knowing that I'd aced the day.

But then — wouldn't you know it? — that tricky *yetzer hara* got me. He did it with a sneak attack, coming up from behind when I wasn't expecting him.

I was in the middle of Shemoneh Esrei, davening up a storm, when I felt something itchy on my leg. A mosquito bite? The itch got worse. I tried to ignore it, but it was driving me crazy. Where had the mosquito come from? What wouldn't I give to scratch it! But I couldn't scratch it during Shemoneh Esrei. I shouldn't even be *thinking* about it during Shemoneh Esrei ....

But I *was* thinking about it during Shemoneh Esrei. In fact, Shemoneh Esrei was just about over, and all I'd been doing for the past few minutes was brooding about that mosquito and the itchy bite that I couldn't scratch.

Failure again.

That night, I lay in bed feeling lower than I'd ever felt in my life.

Anyone who knows me will tell you that Levi Sanders is a kid who succeeds. I'm a top student; I can figure out almost any problem, I can even build scientific contraptions that actually work! But I couldn't seem to get through one day without ruining my perfect record.

Just before I drifted off into an unhappy sleep, I thought about the next day. Tomorrow was Erev Rosh Hashanah. I'd already given up on my dream of one perfect day.

One hour, I thought drowsily.

Tomorrow, I'd try to get through a single hour with perfection. This was it: my last chance.

I was finally going to get it right.

I won't take you through a minute-by-minute account of the first few hours of the day. Suffice it to say that each time, something went wrong. You'd think that sixty short minutes were not too much to ask for, but I couldn't seem to manage even that.

With each passing hour, my heart sank lower. In the early afternoon, my mother served us a light lunch of tuna sandwiches and cut-up veggies. I wasn't very hungry, but I sat down anyway. As I munched my sandwich, I watched the hands of the kitchen clock tick away the minutes. In just a few hours, Rosh Hashanah would be here. Was I ready to be judged? A kid who couldn't manage one perfect month, or one perfect week, or even one perfect day? A kid who was finding it impossible to get through a single *hour* without doing something wrong?

The minute hand of the clock swept past the twelve again. It was one o'clock. A brand-new hour was beginning. I felt a sudden surge of hope. I could do this! Right now, this upcoming hour, could be the one that lifted me over the top!

It was time to *bentch*. Never had I picked up a *bentcher* with such focus. Never did I start saying the words with such intense *kavanah*. This was my hour!

Across the table from me, my little sister Chani was also bentching — out loud. Unfortunately, she didn't know the words very well yet, and she was singing off-tune besides. Her singing was annoying. It was affecting my concentration.

I tried to ignore it, but with each passing second I was growing more and more irritated. Finally, I lowered my *bentcher* and glared at her.

She met my eyes and saw the fury in them. The singing stopped. Her lower lip trembled and her eyes grew shiny. And then Chani opened her mouth and started bawling.

My heart dropped to the floor. I'd made my little sister cry!

I hadn't even said a word. Just one look — one furious glare — and her tender heart had been lacerated. She was crying hard now, big, salty tears that rolled down her cheeks and splashed onto her plate.

Her small shoulders were heaving and she was finding it hard to catch her breath. All because of me.

I wasn't angry at Chani anymore. She was just a little kid. She didn't know any better. But I *was* angry at myself. I was so frustrated and disappointed that *I* could have cried, too.

In fact, about sixty seconds later, I was.

I managed to get to the end of bentching and out of the room before the first tears came. A whole month of letting myself down, of being upset with myself, of feeling like a failure, came pouring out with those tears.

I sat on the plaid loveseat in the den — the closest room to the kitchen — and cried for my lost hope of ever getting it right. Even for just one hour.

My father found me there when he came in a few minutes later. He was home from work early because it was Erev Rosh Hashanah. I rubbed my damp cheeks as he sat next to me on the loveseat. "What's the matter, Levi?"

I considered telling him that nothing was wrong but realized that my red eyes and tear-stained face were a dead giveaway. Besides, at that point I didn't even care if he knew what a failure I was. Letting him know couldn't hurt any worse than knowing it myself ....

So I told him.

I told him about my plans to have a perfect Elul, and then a perfect week, and then a perfect day. I told him about my *yetzer hara*'s amazing ingenuity, and how I'd fallen into its traps every time. I told him about my resolution to have one perfect hour, on this last day before the Day of Judgment. And then I told him about Chani.

He listened patiently, not interrupting me once. When I was done, he nodded as if he understood exactly how I was feeling. "It's not easy," he said.

"You can say that again." I hung my head.

"Here's the thing," Daddy said. "I think you were trying to change too many things at once. It's better to focus your efforts on just one or two areas at a time instead of aiming for perfection. No one is perfect, Levi. You know that, don't you?"

I nodded, though I still secretly wished that *I* could be.

"The Aseres Yemei Teshuvah are coming up," my father continued, one arm lying along the back of the loveseat as though to support me in my misery. "The Ten Days of Repentance. It's a time to express your remorse for all the times you got things wrong."

"I know that, Daddy." I sighed with frustration. "I just wish ..."

"You wish ...?"

"I wish I could go back in time! If I could only start this month over again, I *know* I'd be able to get it right. I could learn from my mistakes! I could get it right, once and for all ...."

To my surprise, my father smiled. "Guess what, Levi? You're going to get your wish."

"I am?"

"Sure. What do you think *teshuvah* does? It turns back the clock. If you really regret doing an *aveirah*, Hashem goes back in time, so to speak, and erases that *aveirah* — as if it never happened!"

I just looked at him. A slow warmth began to spread through me. The first, faint beginnings of comfort.

"And if you do *teshuvah* in the best way — not because you're scared of being punished, but because you love Hashem so much that you don't want to let Him down — then your *aveiros* actually turn into *mitzvos*!" My father smiled at me, offering his words as if they were the greatest gift on earth. Which they were ...

We talked for a long time. And when I finally left that den, I had a different goal.

Instead of concentrating on myself — on *my* perfect record — I was going to shift my focus to Hashem.

Tonight, and for the next two days, I would stand in shul on Rosh Hashanah and proclaim that Hashem was my King. I would let Him know just how much I love Him. And I would hope for His help, so I could become a better person in the coming year.

Not a perfect one, because there's no such thing.

Just a person who's a little better than he was before. Because, after a whole month of trying, I know how hard even *that* can be!

And I know that Hashem will help. Because He loves me, too.

And just as important — He believes in me.

STRAIGHT A'S

"Thanks, Ma. That was a great meal." I pushed my chair back from the table.

Before I was even on my feet, my sister cried, "Adina, it's your turn to do the dishes!"

"I'll clear the table," I said lightly. "I have no time for the dishes; I've got a big test tomorrow."

"Ma-a!" Etti implored. "Tell her!"

My mother heaved a long-suffering sigh. "Girls, remember our deal? The two of you are old enough to divide up the chores between yourselves. And that's exactly what you should do."

"*I* don't complain," I announced as I picked up two plates and started for the kitchen.

"You don't do anything else, either!" Etti said, following me. "You're always using your studying as an excuse."

"It's no excuse. How else do you think I manage to get straight A's?"

"You could still do the dishes," Etti argued, trailing me like a shadow as I returned to the dining room for more plates. "How long would that take?"

"Too long," I told her.

Then, seeing the look on her face, I relented. "Tell you what — I'll bake a cake for Shabbos. A chocolate cake. Okay?"

Etti frowned. "You *like* baking. Why can't you ever do a job that you don't like so much?"

"That," I told her with a wink, "is the secret of a happy life. Turning work into fun!"

Not to be immodest or anything, but I was pretty good at that. In fact, I was great at it! Though I was a diligent student — straight A's, as I'd just told Etti — I still managed to turn schoolwork into fun.

How? There were lots of ways. Study parties, doing homework on the phone with a friend, or giving myself a treat after finishing a particularly hard assignment. Some people think the only way to have fun is by ducking out of your responsibilities. But *I* say there's no reason why life can't be a barrel of fun even if you do everything you're supposed to! It's a knack I've developed over the years, and it stands me in good stead.

"But —"

"Sorry, Etti," I interrupted, depositing the last of the cutlery into the dishpan. "Gotta run. Three of my friends will be here soon to study with me …."

With that, I turned my back on the kitchen — and on my sister's resentful face. Why did she have to argue all the time? I wished she'd relax and learn how to have fun. Like me!

My friends and I had a great time studying that night, and I aced the Chumash test the next morning. I was feeling pretty good as I sauntered down the hall toward my locker at lunchtime, to exchange my morning books for the afternoon ones.

The minute I opened my locker, I noticed something different. I keep my stuff pretty neat in there, so the white envelope sticking out between two textbooks practically punched me in the eye, so to speak. Curious, I pulled it out and lifted the flap.

There was a short note inside. In block letters, it said: SOMEONE NEEDS YOUR HELP.

I stared at the words as if they could explain themselves. But they refused to reveal any more than what they'd already told me.

Someone needed my help?

Who?

And who had left me a note about it?

I looked up and down the hall to see if there was anyone looking my way. I saw nothing suspicious. Whoever had put the note in my locker was either a good actress, or she was making sure to stay out of sight.

There's nothing like a mystery to get the juices flowing. In this personal mystery, the note was Clue #1. As I replaced it in its envelope and tucked the envelope into my knapsack, I wondered excitedly if there would be a follow-up.

Would there be a second clue, to lead me to the mysterious person who'd left me this message ... and, ultimately, to the even more mysterious person who needed my help?

I couldn't wait to find out.

The next day during lunch I tore down the hall toward the lockers. As I opened mine, I realized that I was holding my breath. Would there be another note?

YES! There was the telltale white oblong note, sticking out from between the same two textbooks as the day before. My heart beat faster as I plucked it out. I practically ripped the note to shreds in my eagerness to read it.

SOMEONE NEEDS YOUR HELP, the note said again.

But this time there was a postscript: IF YOU WANT TO HEAR MORE, MEET ME ON THE BASE-

MENT STAIRS AT THE END OF LUNCH BREAK.

I studied the handwriting for a clue as to the writer's identity. But this note, like the first, had been written in block letters.

Why all the mystery? I wondered. I thought of myself as a pretty giving person. Just two nights ago I'd spent hours explaining all the difficult *Rashi*s on our *Chumash* test to my friends. What kind of help did the mystery person need, and why didn't she just come up to me and ask for it?

I was about to find out. In just half an hour, after I'd eaten my lunch, I would slip down to the basement stairs to meet the writer of the mysterious notes.

In my excitement it was hard to swallow a bite. The notes had turned an ordinary trip to my locker into an adventure. And in just minutes I'd be embarking on an even bigger adventure! The noises of the busy school faded behind me as I tiptoed down the stairs toward the basement.

Six steps took me to a curve. Rounding it cautiously, I found myself facing the bottom of the stairwell ... and the back of someone's head.

I hesitated, and then cleared my throat. The girl turned around.

"Chaya!" I said in surprise. In the recent shuffle of the various classes in my grade, Chaya Mann had become a new classmate of mine — though not one that I knew very well yet.

"Hi, Adina," Chaya said calmly. "Thanks for coming."

"Did … did you write me those notes?"

She nodded.

"But … why all the mystery? Why not just come over and talk directly to me?"

"This is a delicate situation," Chaya said solemnly. "There's someone who …"

"Needs my help," I finished impatiently. "That's what you wrote in the notes. Well, who is it? And what kind of help does she need?"

Chaya hesitated. "She'd rather tell you herself. The question is, are you willing to meet her?"

"Sure. We could meet in front of the school later, or —"

"No. The girl wants to meet somewhere else. Some place where people won't see her."

Now I was really intrigued. "Why?"

"That's for *her* to say. Are you willing to meet?"

"Where?"

"In the park near your house. Five-thirty today, on the bench by the fountain."

A thrill ran up my spine. This was just like something out of a spy story. What a blast!

"Sure!" I said. "Uh, can you give me a teensy-weensy hint as to what this is about?"

Chaya Mann shook her head. "Sorry ..."

"Five-thirty, then."

"Right. At the bench by the fountain. Now, I'll leave first. You count to fifty and then follow me back upstairs."

With a finger to her lips, Chaya slipped past me and ran lightly up the stairs. I watched her disappear around the curve of the staircase like a stream of smoke in the wind — or a spy fading into the shadows.

My heart was thudding with almost unbearable excitement as I burst through my front door at 5:15 that afternoon. I planned to dump my knapsack, take a quick drink, and then dash out again to make it to the park on time.

But I hadn't factored in a certain glitch in my plans. A glitch by the name of Etti.

My mother doesn't like when we leave our knapsacks lying around downstairs, so I ran up to deposit mine in my room. I found Etti there, standing in the middle of the room with a feather duster in her hand and a look of indignation on her face.

"There you are!" she said when she saw me. "Have you noticed the way this room looks lately? I keep *my* half neat, but yours is a disaster! How about helping me clean up a little in here?"

"Sorry ... no time." I put down my knapsack and

paused at the mirror to swipe at my hair with a brush.

"What do you mean? There's plenty of time before dinner. If you could at least hang up all your clothes, it would be a start!"

"Etti." I tried to speak patiently, though my blood was racing in my desire to get back outside. "You *know* how I like to operate — let the mess pile up for a couple of weeks, and then have a marathon cleanup session." *With music blasting away in the background and, preferably, a friend or two to keep me company.* "It's more fun that way."

"Fun!" She threw the word at me like a grenade. "Is that all you ever think about, Adina?"

"Of course not ... But why not make a job fun if you can?"

"How about my feelings? Have you ever stopped to think about them? Or about how much I hate living in a pigsty?"

"Oh, come on, Etti. It's not *that* bad ...." I glanced at my watch. It was time to leave if I was going to make it to the park on time.

My sister shook her head. "Don't you ever think about anyone but yourself?" The question sounded more angry than sad.

That stung. "That's not fair."

"Maybe. But it's true."

I shook my head angrily, but I knew that getting into a fight with Etti would only delay me further.

Tersely, I said, "Gotta run. I have to meet someone."

I ran back out of the room before my sister could ask me whom I was meeting. She'd never have believed me if I'd told her that I didn't have a clue ....

The days were longer now, but the sun was beginning to dip toward the horizon by the time I made my way through the park gates. I stopped to scan the scene in front of me.

Just ahead I saw the lake, with the fountain spraying endlessly in its center and a family of black-and-green ducks paddling near the shore. Dotting the paved area around the water were about seven benches, some of them occupied and others empty. I studied them, one by one.

Past the arc of the fountain, on the far bench, I saw a figure that looked about right. As I came closer, I saw that my hunch had been correct: The girl, sitting on the bench with her back to me, was wearing a Bais Yaakov uniform. There was something familiar about the set of her shoulders and the ponytail hanging down her back ... I stepped around to the front of the bench.

"Hi, Adina," Chaya Mann said calmly.

"Chaya! What are *you* doing here?"

"The girl I told you about? She wants me to ... feel things out first." She moved a bag aside and patted the bench beside her. I sat down, feeling a little deflated. I'd been all set to meet the mystery girl.

"So, what's the story?" I asked.

"You remember how I told you that the situation is delicate?"

I nodded.

"Well, here goes ... The girl is a good student, but for some reason this year's math is beyond her. She got an awful mark on her report card last semester, and her parents were very disappointed. They told her she'd get a special reward if she did well on math this semester." Chaya paused. "The problem is, she can't teach it to herself if she doesn't understand it, right?"

"So ... she wants me to teach her the math?" I felt let down. There's nothing more boring than teaching someone how to solve problems that you find perfectly clear. That's why I always prefer to study for math tests either on my own, or in a study party where I can have fun with my friends.

Chaya nodded. "That's it."

I frowned. "Why the big mystery? Why couldn't she just come over and ask me herself?"

"Would you have said 'yes'?"

I hesitated. "I guess I would've invited her to a study party before the next test."

"That's exactly what this girl doesn't want," Chaya said. "She doesn't think she'll be able to learn much in that kind of setting. What she wants — *needs* —

is some one-on-one." She paused, and then asked me again, "Would you have said 'yes' to that?"

"Well … I'm pretty busy these days. I don't know if I have the time …."

"You found the time to come here today," Chaya pointed out.

"This was different."

"How?"

I squirmed on the hard bench. "The whole mystery thing was fun. It made me curious! I was so excited to come and find out what it was all about …."

"And now you feel let down." Chaya said it as a statement, not a question.

"Well …" I didn't really like to admit it.

"You feel let down because tutoring someone in math isn't much fun. Right?"

When I didn't answer right away, she tilted her head and looked me straight in the eye.

"Tell me something, Adina," she said. "Do you ever think about anything except your own fun?"

This sounded so much like my sister's question that I felt a jolt, like electricity, go right through me.

I'm a straight-A student. I learn things pretty quickly. So let me tell you what I learned right then, sitting on the park bench with Chaya Mann in the last of the late-afternoon sun.

I learned about the funny ways that your eyes can see things. I mean the *inner* eyes — not the regular, outside ones.

With my inner eyes, I'd been seeing myself as a kind, generous person. As a person with a knack for making even chores and responsibilities seem like fun!

In short, I'd been seeing myself as a good human being. A human being equal to, or even maybe a teensy bit better, than most of the people around me.

The electrical jolt I felt on that park bench made me suddenly see things with different eyes. My new eyes showed me a person who cared about nothing except making life fun ... for herself!

Sharing the kitchen chores equally with my sister was no fun, so I simply refused to do it.

Cleaning my half of our room didn't appeal to me, so I didn't do that, either.

And teaching someone math — without a party to make it fun — was boring, so I resisted the whole idea.

Not once did I stop to think about the other person. The person I was ignoring in my never-ending search for fun.

All of this took about a minute of hard thinking. I looked up at Chaya.

"I'm sorry," I said humbly. "You can tell whoever it is that of course I'll do it."

I don't know if you know about being humble. How it feels, I mean. *I* sure didn't know until that moment.

Being humble is half about kicking yourself for not being a better person — and half about liking yourself much more than you ever did before. Because now, you know you're working on deserving it. On spreading the light, instead of keeping it all to yourself ...

Chaya smiled at me. "Thanks, Adina." She reached for her bag and pulled out a math book.

My eyes grew wide. I looked from Chaya to the book, and back again. "*You?*"

She nodded. "I'm just no good with numbers. And I really want to do better on the upcoming report card ..."

"Why didn't you just come over and ask me?" I burst out. "Why all the mystery?"

But even as I asked the question, I knew the answer. There was no need for Chaya to say a word.

Mystery ... Excitement ... Fun.

I drew a deep breath. "Okay. Let's get started before the daylight fades ...."

We studied for half an hour, with plans to continue at my house after dinner. Tutoring Chaya in math was just as boring as I'd expected it to be. But this time, I wasn't doing it to have a good time. I was doing it for the pleasure of seeing the light dawn in Chaya's eyes. Of hearing her say, "I get it! I really *get* it now, Adina!"

Maybe, when I got home, I'd turn on that same light in my sister's eyes when I offered to do the dishes. I sure hoped so.

Because having fun may be dandy — but *nothing* beats making the world a brighter place … one person at a time.

TOO-HUMBLE
HESHY

Heshy came out of the school building and looked up the street. Ahead, he saw a familiar figure. Chaim, a classmate, was nearing the corner on his way home.

Heshy hesitated. A quick sprint would catch him up to Chaim. Maybe they could walk home together ….

Or maybe not. What if Chaim was annoyed to see Heshy fall into step beside him as if he had every right to be there? What if he tried to *pretend* he was fine with the idea — while inside he was wishing that Heshy would just go away?

The decision was taken out of Heshy's hands. Chaim reached the corner, where the light had just turned red.

Bored, he turned his head idly to look around — and spotted Heshy standing in front of the school.

"Hey, Heshy!" he called, cupping his hands to his mouth. His beckoning arm finished the sentence for him.

Elated, but still uncertain, Heshy trotted up to join him. He arrived just as the light changed colors again. The two boys crossed the street.

"You live this way, too, don't you?" Chaim asked as they walked along.

Heshy hung back. "Um ... yes, I do. But you don't have to walk with me if you don't want to. I mean, if you'd rather be alone —"

"Alone? Why would I want to be alone?"

"Well, maybe not alone, exactly. You'd just rather be ... with one of your friends."

Chaim stared. "Heshy, are you all right? You sound a little strange."

Heshy flushed. "I just don't want to intrude."

Shaking his head, Chaim murmured, "Like I said — a little strange. Come on." He started walking again.

Relieved, Heshy hurried to catch up. Then he remembered that Chaim hadn't exactly *said* that he wanted Heshy's company. He probably — definitely — would have preferred one of his close friends instead. On the other hand, how could he say that without hurting Heshy's feelings?

Heshy's head was beginning to spin with all of

these speculations. He decided to *act* as if Chaim was fine with him being there, and hope that it was true. They'd be parting ways at Chaim's corner soon enough anyway.

Chaim made small talk as they sauntered along. It was a perfect day for sauntering: neither too hot nor too cold, with a gentle breeze to make you feel glad to be alive. The days were longer now, so the boys didn't have to walk home in the dark the way they did in the winter. Heshy unzipped his jacket and strode along happily.

"So, what do you think about the trip next week?" Chaim asked.

"It sounds great! I can't believe Rebbi's really going to take us there."

"He says it's a reward for a year of work well done. I can't wait!"

"Me, neither. I'll bet everyone in our class feels that way," Heshy declared.

"Not Kalmy," Chaim said. "Didn't you hear him? He announced to anyone who was listening that he has no intention of going on such a 'dumb trip.'"

"Dumb? What makes it dumb? I think it's a fantastic trip!"

Chaim shrugged. "Go ask Kalmy."

Heshy didn't have to ask him. The next morning, before Rebbi walked in, Kalmy made sure to let everyone know just what he thought of the class trip. *They* could go if they wanted to. *He* was going to stay home and relax.

The other boys stared at him in disbelief. Then they went back to discussing the trip.

"My parents said I have to pay for half of it out of my birthday money," Nachman complained.

"Twenty-five dollars! My parents thought it was pretty expensive, too," Dovid said.

Two things happened then: The bell rang, and Rebbi walked into the room. There was a scramble to reach their seats. The school day had officially begun.

But Heshy couldn't get the previous scene out of his mind.

Over and over, he replayed the part where Nachman and Dovid spoke about the expense of the trip. Heshy had happened to be looking in Kalmy's direction at that moment. And what he'd seen troubled him.

As he listened to the other boys talk about how much the trip was going to cost, Kalmy's face had undergone a change. Something had flashed through it — a painful something. A hint of distress. A secret sorrow ...

As Rebbi started his lesson, Heshy continued thinking about Kalmy. He wore nice clothes, but Heshy had noticed that there weren't a whole lot of them. He owned his own bat and ball and glove, but Heshy had seen the great care Kalmy took of them. As if it would be difficult to replace them, should they get lost or damaged ...

Heshy noticed a lot of things. Shy in class and with his classmates, he spent most of his time quietly observing people. He didn't do it in an aloof way, as if he thought he was better than them. On the contrary, Heshy was very humble.

Maybe *too* humble. With a father who demanded a lot from him and two big sisters who could be very critical, he'd learned to keep his head down and try to please everyone. His younger siblings adored him, and there were some boys in his class who would not have minded getting to know him better. But Heshy found it hard to believe that anyone could really be interested in him. Five minutes in his company, he felt, would be enough to make anyone bored of him.

So Heshy kept to himself. He did his work, smiled a lot — and noticed everything.

This morning, he'd noticed the look of pain on Kalmy's face when the trip was discussed. It was a trip that any kid would be eager to take part in. Why wasn't Kalmy?

But maybe the problem wasn't what Kalmy thought of the trip. Maybe the problem was … what the trip would cost.

For a boy whose family didn't have a lot of money, twenty-five dollars could spell the difference between having the time of his life on a fantastic class trip — or staying home and pretending that he'd never really wanted to go in the first place ….

Rebbi's voice continued at the front of the room, but Heshy wasn't listening. He believed he'd hit the nail on the head. Kalmy was pretending that he didn't want to go on the trip, because his parents couldn't afford it.

A puzzled frown settled over Heshy's face. He distinctly remembered Rebbi announcing that any parents who had a problem with the expense of the trip could call him to arrange a discount. Why hadn't Kalmy told his parents about that?

Heshy didn't know the answer. Maybe Kalmy hadn't been paying attention to that part. Or maybe it was something else …

Heshy could have left the whole thing alone. After all, this was not his business. *He* was going on the trip. He'd already handed in his money and was looking forward to it. Why should he care if Kalmy didn't go?

But he did care. He wanted Kalmy to enjoy himself, too. He wanted to erase that fleeting look of pain from Kalmy's face.

Which was why lunchtime found Heshy walking along the connecting walkway that linked the elementary school to the high school building. Kalmy, he knew, had an older brother in high school.

And Heshy had just half an hour to track him down.

"Kalmy Teichman's brother?" the high school boy repeated above the babble in the lunchroom. "I don't know any Kalmy, but I do know a Teichman. There's a Mendy Teichman in the tenth grade. Is that the one you want?"

"I'm not sure," Heshy said humbly. He went over to the tenth-grade table to find out.

Mendy Teichman turned out not to have any younger brothers. But he did point Heshy in the direction of a group of eleventh-graders eating lunch at a table along the far wall. "You could try them. I think there's another Teichman in that grade."

There *was* another Teichman. And, to Heshy's relief, it was the right Teichman.

"Kalmy?" repeated his brother, Reuven. "You're here with a message from Kalmy?"

"No," Heshy said patiently. "I'm here with a message *about* Kalmy. Is ... is there someplace where we can talk privately?"

Curious, the older boy led Heshy to a quiet corner of the big lunchroom. "Okay, shoot."

"Well ... it's like this." Heshy began by telling Reuven about the class trip his rebbi had organized for the following week. "The trip costs a lot — twenty-five dollars. But there's a discount for parents who call our rebbi."

Reuven frowned. "I haven't heard Kalmy talk about the trip at home."

"He … he says he's not going. He claims he wants to stay home because it's a 'dumb trip.'" Heshy met Reuven's eyes earnestly. "But I don't think that's true. I think he wants to go. I think it's the money that's the problem …."

He held his breath, hoping that Reuven would forgive him for being so pushy. He didn't want to intrude on the Teichmans' personal business. He just wanted to erase that look from Kalmy's face ….

"I see," Reuven said thoughtfully. He hesitated, and then made a decision to share something with Heshy. "Things have been tight at our house since our father lost his job. I guess Kalmy didn't want to bother my parents about money for a school trip."

"But with the discount …"

"Maybe Kalmy didn't want to put our parents to the bother, or the embarrassment, of asking for one." Reuven's face wore a determined look. "I'll see what I can do."

"Thanks a lot!" Heshy beamed.

Reuven was about to say something else when he was interrupted by the harsh blare of the bell above their heads. Someone called his name from the table he'd abandoned.

"That means my lunch break is over, too," Heshy gasped. "Bye!"

And he was off like the wind.

As he dashed down the walkway, he was beset by

visions of irate teachers and unexcused late notes. But none of that really mattered to him. He was feeling too uplifted by what had just happened. He'd tracked down Kalmy's big brother and spoken to him about the trip — and Reuven had said he'd take care of it. What could be better than that?

Heshy *was* late for class, and he did have to shuffle down to the office for a note and a scolding. Normally, that would have upset him. But right then, he was feeling far too contented to care.

The next day, Rebbi collected the last of the trip fees from those students who'd forgotten to bring it the day before. To Heshy's secret delight, Kalmy came up to the desk with an envelope of his own.

"I thought you weren't planning to go?" someone stage-whispered as Kalmy passed him.

Kalmy shrugged. "Changed my mind."

But Heshy, surreptitiously observing Kalmy, saw a flash of something in his eyes. Something happy …

He spent the rest of the morning trying to catch up on the Gemara that he'd missed the day before, when he'd been busy brooding about Kalmy. Today his mind was clear and he could focus. He paid attention and asked a question or two. By the time the bell rang for lunch, he was almost caught up.

Feeling satisfied with his morning's work, Heshy

followed his classmates down to the lunchroom. He sat at the end of the table as usual, not expecting anyone to talk to him and telling himself that he didn't really care if anyone did. He was munching his sandwich in his customary silence when he felt a sudden, sharp jab in his ribs. The boy next to him had nudged him.

"Hey, Heshy! See that high school kid — Kalmy's brother? He's been talking to Kalmy. And now I hear he's looking for *you*!"

Heshy looked up to see Reuven Teichman bearing down on him.

"Hi, Heshy," Reuven said easily. Heshy could sense the awe rippling up and down the table. A high school kid — a popular one — had come over to the middle school to seek out Heshy! He sat up straighter, conscious of the crimson crawling up from his collar to his cheeks. "Any place we can talk?"

Wordlessly, Heshy got to his feet, grabbed his lunch bag, and led Reuven to a corner of the big room.

"I didn't get a chance to thank you yesterday," Reuven said when they were out of earshot of the others. "You ran away too fast."

"Uh, that's all right." Heshy felt like a fool, standing there clutching his brown paper bag. "I just wanted to help."

"I didn't tell Kalmy what you did," Reuven continued. "I told my father the whole story, and he called your rebbi to arrange the money for the trip. He pretended that he found out about the trip when the rebbi called him to find out why Kalmy wasn't going."

"I'm sure Rebbi would have done that in a day or two anyway," Heshy mumbled.

"But you got there first. You saved my brother from feeling bad for another couple of days." Reuven studied the younger boy. "You know, I mentioned your name to Kalmy — casually, as if I'd just happened to bump into you the other day. And he said something that I found very interesting."

The buzz of voices in the lunchroom sounded distant, like the roar of a faraway ocean. Heshy was intensely embarrassed — but also curious. "What?" he asked.

"He said that you've been in his class for two years now, but he hardly knows you at all. He says you're always super-quiet. That you don't say much." Reuven gazed at him. "But you *see* a lot. Don't you?"

Heshy didn't know what to say. He nodded.

"And you care a lot, too. Right?"

"Um ..."

"I know you do. Or you wouldn't have taken the trouble to hike all the way over to the other building and spend your whole lunch period tracking me down and convincing me to help Kalmy." Reuven smiled. "You're a good kid, Heshy. Why won't you admit that?"

"Er ..."

"I'm not asking you to be conceited or anything.

But *not* thinking well enough of yourself is also a problem." He paused. "Kalmy says you seem to not have that many friends. Frankly, for such a nice kid, I find that a little hard to believe!"

Heshy looked down at his feet. He wished Reuven would go away. It had been nice of him to come over to say "thank you" for Heshy's help. But that was enough. It was more than enough.

Reuven apparently thought otherwise. "You've got to *really* see yourself, Heshy," he urged. "A kid who sees what other kids are feeling, and who actually gets up and *does* something about it … Well, don't you think a kid like that deserves some friends?"

Put that way, it did make a certain amount of sense. Before Heshy could think of a way to answer, he was saved by the bell.

"Well, thanks again, Heshy," Reuven said.

"Thank you, too …," Heshy managed.

Reuven grinned. "You know what they say — one good turn deserves another. Just think over what I said. I think you'll find out that it's true."

Heshy did think it over. He thought it over as he returned to the table to *bentch*, trying to ignore his classmates' curious stares and whispers. He thought about it all through his afternoon classes. And he was still thinking about it when he emerged from the school building and saw Chaim standing at the corner up ahead.

Heshy hesitated — but only for a second. Then he ran.

"Hi!" he called breathlessly.

Chaim turned. "Oh, hi, Heshy." He smiled. "Want to walk home together?"

It was on the tip of Heshy's tongue to ask, "If you're sure I'm not intruding …?"

Instead he drew a deep breath, and all he said was, "Sure …"

The two boys fell in step. Chaim said, "Well, that's a first! I was getting bored of always having to convince you that I actually *enjoy* your company."

With a startling flash of insight, like a bolt of lightning that illuminates a dark landscape, Heshy realized that his fear of boring others really *did* come true — when he spent all his time worrying about boring others!

Otherwise, there was really no reason to be afraid. No reason at all …

"It's boring for me, too." Heshy spoke lightly, because his heart was feeling light. But old habits die hard. He hesitated a long moment before daring to utter his next words. "Uh … Chaim?"

"Yeah?"

"Do you want to come over and play basketball in my backyard? The days are longer now, and —"

"You don't have to convince me, Heshy. You're on!" Chaim's pace quickened. "I've never even seen you play. Are you any good?"

Humble Heshy wanted to shrug off the question. But Honest Heshy broke into a big grin and said, "Actually, I shoot a pretty mean hoop! I practice a lot." It's easy to find lots of time to practice when you have no friends to speak of.

"Can we practice together?" Chaim asked eagerly. "I don't have a hoop at home."

Being humble was fine, Heshy thought. But he'd had gone *way* beyond humble. He'd gone into a place — a lonely place — where he was all alone for no reason on earth, with a heart that was chock-full of good feelings but no one to benefit from them.

"No problem," he said happily, as he rounded the corner onto his own block — and into a whole new life.

HAPPY ENDINGS

I t had rained recently, and the woods that edged the farm were dank and uninviting. Water dripped off branches, falling on the head of the girl slipping silently through the trees like a shadow or a breath of wind.

Gita Werner was ten years old. She wore the faded dress she always put on for doing the chores, and sturdy work boots that didn't mind mud or dirt. Under her arm she carried a small shoebox, a souvenir from the last time her mother had been able to afford to buy her a new pair of shoes. Inside the box was Gita's most precious possession: her diary.

On she walked. To someone watching her, it might have seemed as if she were merely meandering through the woods. But this was no random stroll. Gita knew exactly where she was going. And, a few minutes later, she was there.

It was a tiny clearing among the trees. If the sun had been shining, it would have created a small patch of golden warmth right where she stood. Gita loved this spot. This was where she came whenever she had a few spare minutes. She would always bring her diary along and spend a few delicious minutes scribbling on its pages.

Gita adored writing. Mostly, she wrote stories that she made up at night when she couldn't sleep. But sometimes — like today — her heart was so heavy inside her that she just had to spill some of that weight onto the diary's blank sheets. She sat down on a slightly damp rock, took a pencil stub from her pocket and the diary from its box, and started writing.

Dear Diary,

This is it — the last day. Tomorrow, Mama and I will be loading our suitcases into Farmer Brown's truck and leaving the farm behind forever.

Mama tried. She really did. Ever since Papa died, she's done her very best to keep the farm going. But we've had so much bad luck. Drought, insects, poor crops ... Mama says there's simply not enough money for us to live here anymore, and she won't live on charity. For a long time after Papa died, some of our neighbors helped us out with food, but Mama won't do that anymore. She says we have to leave.

We're going to live with Mama's Cousin Ella, in a big city called New York. I don't know if I'll like it there. Mama says it'll be very different from the farm. She says I'll go to school and make friends. When I asked her if it will be a Jewish school, she looked worried and said she didn't know. Mama looks worried all the time these days. Worried and sad. I'd do anything to make her smile again, the way she used to. But I don't know how.

Gita paused a moment, gazing off into the gloom beyond the tree line. *She* was worried, too. She'd never met Cousin Ella or Ella's family. She wondered if she'd make friends in the big city, as Mama had promised. It wouldn't really matter if she didn't, she thought. She was used to being alone. Gita was an only child, and for a long time now it had been just the two of them — Mama and her. Still, a friend would be nice ....

She bent her head over the diary and wrote again.

I like to make up stories. It's fun creating something brand-new where there was nothing be-fore. Mama says that the Almighty made the whole world, so I guess He's the best Storyteller of all. If I were writing the story of my life, I wouldn't know

how to make the ending come out happy. But I bet
He would. The Almighty knows how to do every-
thing. So I guess I'll have to leave it up to Him.

One again, she paused to stare sightlessly into the woods. When she resumed her writing, her hand moved more slowly, as if the words were causing her pain.

This will be the last time I'll be writing in you,
dear diary. There are only two blank pages left, so
I'd have had to stop soon anyway. But my whole
life will be changing tomorrow, so I guess it makes
sense to stop here.
I'm going to leave you behind in my very fa-
vorite place in the world. Whenever I think of the
farm and the first ten years of my life, I'll think of
you, dear diary. Even if I can't be here anymore, at
least you will.

She couldn't think of anything more to say. What *could* she say? Mama didn't talk much these days, and Gita couldn't really blame her. Sometimes, sadness went too deep for words.

She closed the diary and sat looking at it for a long moment. Then, with a tiny sigh, she put the diary in the box, closed the lid, and started to dig.

With the ground so moist, the soil was loose and easy to move. Gita's hands — and her dress — were soon covered in mud, but she didn't care. When she'd dug a shallow hole, she tenderly placed the box inside and covered it up again.

She felt as if she were burying a piece of her own heart.

The story of Gita Werner's life in the big city was one that she could never have made up. That was because it was so unimaginably different from everything she'd known before.

First of all, the houses were different: ugly red brick instead of the weathered wood of the farmhouse. Surrounding the houses was hard cement pavement instead of pastures and woods. Even the air felt different: a little stale, like the air inside a box.

Cousin Ella was different, too. She didn't even light Shabbos candles, and she laughed when Mama lit hers. It was not a pleasant, sharing-a-joke-together kind of laugh, but one as ugly as the brick house in which she and Uncle Irving and Gita's cousins lived.

The big public school Gita attended was very different from the little school she'd gone to before. There, she'd known everyone and everyone had known her. Here she was just another face among hundreds of strange faces. She was so shy that it took her a long time to make a friend.

Eventually, she did make one. And then some

more. By this time she was twelve years old and growing more confident in her new surroundings. If Mama was even more quiet than usual these days, Gita — who was now called Gail — didn't notice. She was busy with her new friends, and with all the interesting new things there were to do and see in the big city. Soon she became a teenager and was even busier. She didn't realize how pale her mother was, or hear the hacking cough that Mama had developed in her job as a sewing-machine operator in a big factory.

But she did notice when her dear Mama breathed her last.

She cried for a whole week, as people drifted in and out of the house to pay their respects. When she returned to school, she was almost as pale as her mother had been at the end.

But Gail was young, and all of life was ahead of her. Her new friends consoled her and kept her distracted. Cousin Ella approved of Gail's friends, and encouraged them to drop in after school and on weekends. Gail was soon living such a whirlwind life that she hardly had time to remember what had come before.

It was only in the small hours of the night, when she couldn't sleep, that she thought of her Mama and felt a tear trickle down her cheek in the dark.

Gail's daughter, Faye, hardly ever cried. From the

day she was born she was full of gaiety and fun. And why not? She'd been born into a comfortable home. Her father was a doctor and her mother was beautiful and exciting. Faye grew up charming, but rather self-centered. When she was old enough to be thinking of marriage, she was determined to marry someone rich and handsome.

The man she eventually married *was* rich, and handsome, too. Unfortunately, he had hardly any conception of what it meant to be a Jew. Faye's mother, Gail, had lit Shabbos candles every Friday night, but Faye turned her back on that old-fashioned custom the minute she had a home of her own.

She and her husband lived life in the fast lane. They boarded jets the way other people boarded buses. They flew all over the world, and when they weren't flying they were entertaining friends at their opulent home. Their daughter, Linda, grew up wondering what it would be like to have a mother who actually tucked you in at night ….

Linda was a quiet girl. She hardly made any trouble for her busy mother and father — for which they were grateful. In return, they bought her lots of expensive presents and blew kisses at her as they walked out the door. Linda felt sad sometimes, and she tried to forget her sadness by reading books. She eagerly looked forward to her visits to the library.

One day, she took an interesting-looking book out

of the library. It was about a Jewish family. She knew that she was Jewish, too — but there the resemblance ended. The things the book-family did, and the things they said and thought and felt, seemed a world away from the way things were in her own home. Linda was confused.

In an attempt to figure things out, she took out more books about Jewish families. As she grew older, she branched out into books about Jewish ideas. It was no coincidence that she struck up a friendship with the old couple that lived at the end of their block. The couple had a married son who sometimes brought his children over to visit. Those children looked a lot like the girls and boys in the books Linda had read. Talking to them and their parents opened up a whole new world for her.

One thing led to another, and by the time Linda was fifteen she had joined a group especially designed for girls like her. Girls who knew they were Jewish but wanted to know much more. Girls like Linda, who had everything they wanted but wanted something else. Girls who had a thirst that water couldn't quench.

Linda made friends in this group, and they were very different from the friends she'd made in the exclusive private school to which her parents had sent her. Together, they made the fantastic journey toward the place they were so eager to learn about. The place where they had come from. The place where they belonged …

Some years later, all of Linda's friends from the group came to dance at her wedding.

Linda — who was now called Leah — felt a little sorry for her parents, who seemed bewildered by all the changes in her life. They didn't know what to make of her new lifestyle, or of the serious young yeshivah student who had just become her new husband.

As for Leah herself, she couldn't have been happier.

It had rained recently, and the woods that edged the campgrounds were dank and uninviting. Nevertheless, Gitty decided to go exploring, in the hopes of finding the "colored leaf" she needed for the scavenger hunt.

Her friend Michal was with her. She peered doubtfully into the trees. "It sure looks wet in there. Are you sure you want to go in?"

"We need to find a leaf that's already changed color. There's a better chance of finding one in the woods than anywhere else."

"Maybe they haven't changed color yet."

"It's the end of August, Michal. Fall's around the corner. C'mon, let's check it out."

Gitty led the way. Her shoes quickly became damp, but she didn't care. Here and there, she spotted a leaf on the ground that seemed a bit brighter than its fellow leaves. But she wanted to find a really colorful one.

"Just a little further," she urged.

They reached a tiny clearing among the trees. If the sun had been shining, it would have created a small patch of golden warmth right where she was standing. Gitty shivered with delight. What a perfect spot!

"Here's a leaf!" Michal stooped to the ground to pick it up. It was red and orange, with faint overtones of yellow. "We'd better get back."

Gitty was gazing rapturously around her. "Isn't this a great place for a picnic?"

"A bit too damp for my taste …" Michal shivered. It was cool under the trees.

"I don't mean *now*. On a sunny day, we could spread a blanket right here" — she gestured at the center of the clearing — "and bring …" Her voice trailed off as something caught her eye. "Hey, what's that?"

At first, she'd taken the splotch of crimson for just another leaf. Moving closer, she saw that it was not a leaf at all. In fact, it had never been alive. What Gitty was looking at was the corner of a red box. Most of it was buried beneath the soil, but the heavy rains had apparently washed away some of the earth to expose this corner.

"Leave it alone," Michal begged. "It's just an old box! Let's go back, Gitty. I'm cold."

"One second …" Gitty crouched over the box,

took hold of the exposed corner, and carefully tugged. There was little resistance as the box slipped out of the dark earth.

"What …?" It looked like a shoebox small enough to hold a child's shoes. Gingerly, Gitty lifted the lid. Inside was a small book with a fake leather cover.

She picked it up and read the words embossed in faded gilt letters on the front: MY DIARY.

"It's a diary," Gitty breathed.

Michal was at her shoulder, staring with equal fascination at her friend's find. "Who do you think buried it there?"

Gitty shrugged. She opened the cover. On the fly-leaf, in a young, careful handwriting, were the words "Gita Werner."

A strange chill ran up Gitty's spine.

Most people thought that "Gitty" was short for "Gittel." But she knew better. She knew that it was short for "Gita."

When she was born, her mother had researched the family tree and discovered the name of Gitty's great-grandmother. Not much was known about her, except her name and the fact that she'd come over from Europe with her parents when she was only a baby, and lived in upstate New York for a while before moving to the big city ….

Gitty turned the page. The writing was so faded as to be almost illegible now. She felt a pang; she'd have liked to read the writing of the unknown girl who shared her name. Turning more pages, she saw paragraphs here and there that were better preserved than the rest. She would take the diary back to the bunk, she decided, and see what she could make of it.

In the distance, they heard the camp loudspeaker signaling the end of the scavenger hunt. It was time to go back. Quickly, she flipped to the last written page.

The words seemed to jump out at her, surprisingly readable:

Mama says that the Almighty made the whole world, so I guess He's the best Storyteller of all. If I were writing the story of my life, I wouldn't know how to make the ending come out happy. But I bet He would. The Almighty knows how to do every-thing. So I guess I'll have to leave it up to Him.

Gitty's heart twisted with feeling for the unknown girl who had written those words.

Feeling strangely touched, without knowing why, she tucked the old diary into her pocket and turned to go.

And somewhere far beyond the woods — far beyond the whole world — another girl named Gita was looking down at her, and laughing.

She was laughing with joy — because the Creator of all stories had brought about a happy ending to the story of her life.

Just as she'd never, ever stopped believing that He would.

GLOSSARY

Achdus — unity

Aliyah, aliyos — being called up to make the blessings on the Torah reading

Aseres Yemei Teshuvah — the Ten Days of Repentance, from Rosh Hashanah to Yom Kippur

Aveirah, aveiros — sin(s)

Bais Yaakov — Orthodox Jewish girls' school

Bar mitzvah — age of thirteen, when a Jewish male becomes obligated to observe the Torah commandments

Baruch Hashem — thank the Almighty

Bas mitzvah — age of twelve, when a Jewish female becomes obligated to observe the Torah commandments

Bentch (Yidd.) — recite Grace After Meals

Bentcher (Yidd.) — booklet containing the text of Grace
  After Meals

Bli neder — without promising

Bnos — girls' activity groups

Brachah, brachos — blessing(s)

Bubby (Yidd.) — grandmother

Chas v'shalom — Heaven forbid

Chavrusa (Aram.) — Torah study partner

Chazal — the Sages

Cholent (Yidd.) — traditional Jewish stew

Chumash — the Bible

Chuppah — wedding canopy

Daven (Yidd.) — pray

Davening (Yidd.) — prayers; praying

Eibishter (Yidd.) — Hashem, the Most High

Eisav — Esau, brother of Jacob, our forefather

Elul — the last month of the Jewish year

Erev Shabbos — Friday

Frum (Yidd.) — religiously observant

Gabbai — manager of the prayers in the synagogue

Gemara (Aram.) — the Talmud; a Talmud volume

Goyim — non-Jews

Hakadosh Baruch Hu — the Holy One, Blessed be He

Hashem — the Almighty

Hashgachah — Divine providence

Hatzoloh — volunteer Jewish ambulance corps

Havdalah — blessing recited at the end of the Sabbath

Kavanah — intent, concentration

Kehillah — congregation

Klal Yisrael — the Jewish people

Kohanim — Jewish priests

Lag B'Omer — the 33rd day of the Omer count between Passover and Shavuos

Lashon hara — gossip

Limudei kodesh — religious studies

Maariv — evening prayer

Masechta (Aram.) — section of the Talmud

Middah, middos — character trait(s)

Minyan — quorum of ten adult Jewish men required for public prayers

Mitzvah, mitzvos — Torah commandment(s)

Motzei Shabbos — Saturday night

Mussar — character improvement

Nachas — satisfaction

Negel vasser (Yidd.) — ritual hand washing

Pareve (Yidd.) — neither meat nor dairy

Rashi — comments by Rabbi Shlomo Yitzchaki, one of the most well-known and extensively studied Torah commentators

Rav — rabbi

Rebbetzin (Yidd.) — rabbi's wife

Rebbi — Torah teacher

Rosh Chodesh — the beginning of a month on the Jewish calendar

Rosh Hashanah — the Jewish New Year

Shabbaton — special program that takes place on the Sabbath

Shabbos — the Sabbath

Shacharis — morning prayers

Seder — Torah study session

Sefer, sefarim — Torah book(s)

Seudah — meal

Shalosh seudos — the third meal on the Sabbath

Shemoneh Esrei — central prayer in Jewish liturgy

Shevatim — the twelve Jewish tribes

Shiur — Torah class

Shtetl (Yidd.) — small Jewish village

Shul (Yidd.) — synagogue

Siddur — prayer book

Tallis — prayer shawl

Talmid chacham, talmidei chachamim — Torah sage(s)

Tatty (Yidd.) — Daddy

Tefillah — prayer

Tefillin — phylacteries, small black boxes containing scrolls with certain Torah portions, worn by adult Jewish males during prayer

Teshuvah — repentance

Torah — the Bible

Tzitzis — fringes worn on the corners of a four-cornered garment by Jewish males

Yaakov Avinu — Jacob, our forefather

Yarmulke (Yidd.) — skullcap

Yid, Yidden (Yidd.) — Jew(s)

Yiddishkeit (Yidd.) — Judaism

Yeshivah — Torah school

Yetzer hara — the evil inclination

Yom tov — a Jewish holiday

Zeidy (Yidd.) — grandfather